THE GIRL IN AREA ONE

A MACY ELLIS PUGET SOUND MYSTERY

BOOK ONE

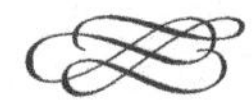

EVA BLUE

DARKNESS AND LIGHT PUBLISHING

A NOTE TO THE READER

While many locations in this book are true to life, some details of the settings have been changed or borrowed from my husband's novels, *The Thomas Austin Crime Thrillers*.

Gonzo is the only character who's real, her mannerisms taken from our dog Buffy, who my daughter named after the vampire slayer.

I have to admit that Macy's mother and father are exaggerated caricatures that resemble my parents. I couldn't imagine more entertaining and endearing folks than my own. Any other resemblances between characters in this book and actual people is purely coincidental.

One more note: after editing and helping plot stories with my husband, D.D. Black, for over a decade, I have learned a lot. But I could not have created this book without his encouragement and help.

It has been a lot of fun creating worlds—both fictional and real life—with this man.

Oh, and one more, one more note: I want to thank my family and friends, my coworker family, and my patients and their families, too. You all inspire me and give my life meaning.

I am so grateful.

Thanks for reading,

Eva Blue

"Let us never consider ourselves finished nurses... we must be learning all of our lives."

-Florence Nightingale

"So much to do, so little done, such things to be."

-Elizabeth Taylor

"Mystery is something that appeals to most everybody."

-Angela Lansbury

PART I
ASSESSMENT, DIAGNOSIS, AND INTERVENTION

Mirth Airport
Shunk Bay
NE Twin Spits Rd
Hansville
Puget Sound
Hood Canal
NE Eglon Rd
Hansville Rd NE
Little Boston Rd NE
Port Gamble
Port Gamble S'Klallam Reservation
NE Little Boston Rd
Port Gamble Bay
Port Gamble Rd NE
NE Wyant Rd
NE Barry St
Kingston Ferry Terminal
Kingston
Thompson Airport Airstrip
Stottlemeyer Rd NE
Big Valley Rd NE
NE Sawdust Hill Rd
NE Gunderson Rd
Miller Bay Rd NE
NE Lincoln Rd
Poulsbo
Front St NE
Port Madison Indian Reservation
Indianola
Suquamish
Port Madison Bay

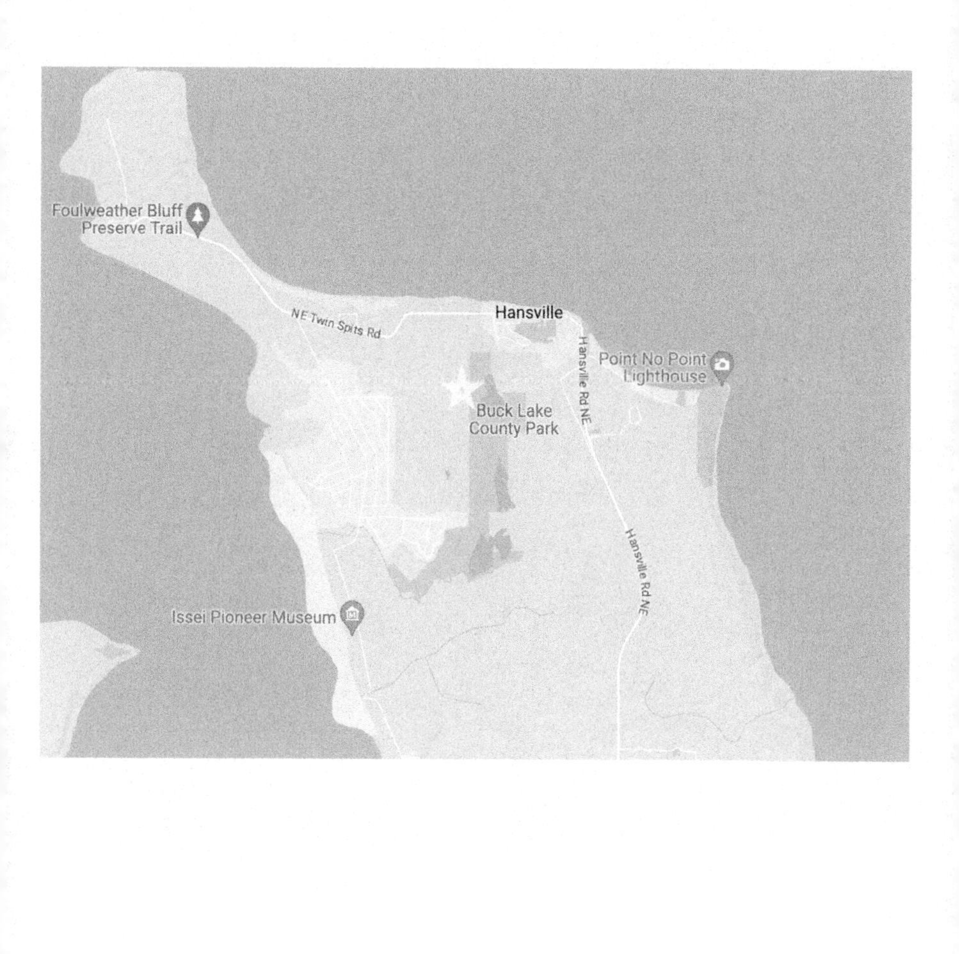
Foulweather Bluff
Preserve Trail
NE Twin Spits Rd
Hansville
Hansville Rd NE
Point No Point
Lighthouse
Buck Lake
County Park
Hansville Rd NE
Issei Pioneer Museum

CHAPTER 1

Hansville, Washington
Western Puget Sound

I'D HAD A ROUGH YEAR, and it was about to get worse.

Red, white, and blue lights pierced my sleep, jolting me awake. My eyes snapped open and I squinted at the red glow of my alarm clock.

3:18 AM

A police siren blasted, then stopped abruptly. Its echo reverberated through my tiny beach house, making my heart race and transforming my confusion into fear.

I rolled up and out of the permanent indentation my body had worn into my twenty-year-old bed. The first-generation memory foam mattress couldn't remember a damned thing.

I floundered through my bedroom, keeping low to the ground. The floor was littered with a week's worth of dirty clothes and, in my groggy state, I tripped over a laundry basket. Adrenaline pumping through my veins, I stumbled out of my bedroom, cursing under my breath.

Grabbing the baseball bat I kept near the door, I peered

through the front window. The flashing lights of emergency vehicles painted the wet street in a kaleidoscope of amber and blue.

Chaos was unfolding at Bob's house. My heart sank as I watched the paramedics wheel out a stretcher carrying a shiny black body bag. I knew without a doubt it was Bob, my ninety-six-year-old neighbor who lived next door.

My house previously belonged to my grandmother. I moved in twenty years ago with my soon-to-be ex-husband, Kenny, when my grandmother needed help and moved in with my mother, who lives six miles away.

When I was young, I was afraid of Bob. He was quiet and kept to himself. As an adult, Bob no longer scared me, but he was still quiet and kept to himself. I knew nothing about the man even though I had known him for over four decades. He had probably lived in this house next to my grandmother for decades before I was even born.

The last time I saw Bob alive was just a week ago. I came home to the old man dangling halfway up a tree using a leather belt and his spiked tree-climbing shoes, no safety harness or ropes. An old chainsaw dangled from the rope tied to his belt. "What are you doing?" I had yelled. "Don't you know I'm off duty? Don't make me come over there and be your nurse." I had worked in geriatrics for a decade and loved to see folks over ninety kicking ass and taking names. But seeing Bob thirty feet in the air and wielding a chainsaw scared the hell out of me.

"Kid, I'm ninety-six," he'd said. "Never needed a nurse before and I ain't gonna need one today. You'd be needing a roofing company if this branch had come down. And, *you'd* be the one needing a nurse if it came through at the wrong time."

Now, as I watched the paramedics parade him across his well-manicured lawn, I was overcome with guilt and sadness, realizing I hadn't thought to check on him in the past few days. Or, come to think of it, ever.

I opened the door and stepped outside, the chilly night air nipping at my skin. The hum of the firetruck, ambulance, and police car engines drowned out the soft lapping of waves I would otherwise hear coming from the shore of the beach fifty feet from my house.

I was still wearing my pajamas, but I didn't care. I needed to see what had happened. I approached one of the paramedics while still clutching my baseball bat.

“Was it Bob?” I asked. “The old man who lives here?”

He nodded. “Little dog was barking its head off for the last four hours. Neighbors knocked on the door, but no one answered. They gave us a call asking us to do a wellness check. By the time we found him, it was too late. Looks like natural causes.”

I thought I recognized the paramedic, but couldn’t quite place him. He was tall, with wavy brown hair. He looked fit but not like someone who would win a bodybuilding contest.

"Wait a minute, Macy?” His eyes widened in recognition. “Macy Ellis? You married Kenny after college, right?”

The sound of Kenny’s name was like a mosquito biting at my ear. I wanted to swat it away, then crush it between my hands with a hate-filled clap. Twelve months ago, Kenny fled to Florida after steering our auto body shop, The Wrench King, off a financial cliff and stealing enough painkillers from my patients to get my nursing license suspended. In the grand scheme of things, I was lucky. I was healthy, lived in a beautiful place, and always had enough of everything that mattered. Even so, looking at this past year—and thinking about Kenny—I had some beef with luck I wished to address. And luck had better watch its back.

I could feel my cheeks burning as I leaned the bat against the fence, and not only because of the cute paramedic’s mention of my ne'er-do-well husband. I self-consciously pulled closed the light purple polyester robe I’d slept in. At ankle’s length I hoped it would cover my worn-out sweatpants turned pajama bottoms and ragged t-shirt. I tied the sash around my waist. "Yeah, that's me. Separated from Kenny now. I didn't recognize you at first. Uhhhh...?"

"Jason," he said with a grin, his dark eyes crinkling at the corners. "Jason Carter. We had a couple classes together, remember?"

My mind reeled back to high school. Suddenly, I could see the younger version of Jason, all gangly limbs and awkward charm. I tossed my hair back in an unconsciously seductive maneuver and smiled. "Oh, right! Jason, of course!" I was trying to sound casual while internally berating myself for inadvertently flirting at such an inappropriate time. "So, you're a paramedic now?"

"Yeah," he said, nodding. "And from what I remember, you became a journalist, right?"

"I was a crime reporter for a while, across the water." I nodded in the general direction of Seattle, which lay about twenty miles to the southeast, on the other side of the Puget Sound. "Now I'm a nurse." I shifted uncomfortably, feeling the weight of my recent suspension. "Well, I'm kind of in between jobs right now," I admitted, avoiding his gaze.

Before he could reply, one of Jason's colleagues emerged from Bob's house, struggling to hold on to a small, growling dog. The animal was clearly agitated, writhing and whining. It was holding something in its mouth.

"What's going to happen to the dog?" I asked, concerned.

"He'll spend the night at the station, then we'll take him to the pound, I guess," Jason replied, shrugging. "What's the dog's name?"

"I don't even know," I answered. I had seen Bob's little black and white Chihuahua mix running around the yard often over the last few years, usually barking, and *always* shivering. The poor little thing even shivered on warm days, which made me think it was a nervous condition, not a lack of padding. But I'd never heard Bob call him by name. And I'd never asked. "I'm a terrible neighbor."

Feeling guilty for not being a better member of the community and a sudden wave of sympathy for the scrappy dog, I offered to take him for the night. I explained that I would bring him to the pound the next day. Jason hesitated, then agreed, and motioned for his colleague to bring the dog.

"He's better off here than in a cage at the station," Jason said.

The other paramedic handed the tiny pup over the waist-high white picket fence. As soon as he was in my arms, he dropped what was in his mouth and nipped at my hand, not hard enough to draw blood, but enough to make his displeasure known. I winced and placed him on the ground, watching as the little beast darted up the porch steps, through my open door, and into my house.

"Are you okay?" Jason asked.

I let him take my hand, and he gently inspected it for injury.

"No blood," I said, trying to ignore the sting of the bite. "Don't worry about me. I'll take care of the dog tonight and I can sort things out tomorrow. It's the least I can do for Bob."

I bent down to pick up whatever the little dog had dropped.

"Ew. Um, you might want to take this and put it with Bob's body," I said, handing Jason what appeared to be Bob's upper denture.

Jason shook his head. "Little guy probably took out the teeth trying to wake up his friend."

I thought of what the dog might be finding in my home to carry in its mouth. Likely dirty laundry.

"Bummer that you had to find Bob dead," I said. "Here you thought you were going to ask him to keep his dog quiet and instead, *this*."

"This is nothing. Natural causes are the only sort of death

scenes I can stand to be called to. This is the least sad thing I've seen this shift."

That stopped me in my tracks. "Did someone else die?"

"Worse."

The word *worse* hit me like a punch to the gut. I imagined a car accident, maybe a pile up. "Can you share what happened?"

"Not allowed to let anyone in on the details. You're a nurse. You know, I'm sworn to HIPAA privacy and all that. And there's an ongoing investigation. Cops aren't saying much yet."

"I get it," I whispered.

Jason's face darkened. "Yeah, it's been a tough night." His eyes met mine and his tone took on a directness it hadn't had before. "Lock your door tonight, okay?"

A chill ran down my spine. I wondered what he wasn't telling me. What he *couldn't* tell me.

I assured him I would, and we exchanged a few more words before Jason left in the ambulance. The fire trucks pulled away, too, leaving the street in silence and me feeling more alone than ever.

I went inside, closed and locked the door behind me, set down the baseball bat, and caught my reflection in the hallway mirror. My hair was a mess, and my threadbare teal t-shirt with neon pink puff lettering that gave a shout out to *Apple Blossom '95*—although a throwback to some good times—was hardly flattering. A large coffee stain that splattered the front of my robe was a glaring reflection of my current life state, something I hoped Jason hadn't noticed through the flashing lights. A pang of embarrassment washed over me. For most of my life, I wouldn't have let anyone see me looking so disheveled.

But, like I said, it had been a rough year. Twenty years of marriage gone in a flash, with little to show for it but mountains of debt and a case pending before the nursing review board. The only good thing left of our marriage was Bridget, the daughter we raised together.

I sighed, disgusted at my embarrassment over how I looked. My neighbor had just died, not to mention whatever other tragedy Jason had been hinting at, and here I was worrying about my looks.

I grabbed my laptop and scrolled the local Facebook groups, looking for news, but so far, nothing had come out that would explain Jason's concern. I considered calling my mom—she was always the first to know what was going on in the community—but it was around four in the morning and there was no way she was up. I'd have to wait.

Pushing the thought aside, I focused on the task at hand. Bob's dog had disappeared somewhere inside my house, and I needed to find him.

"Here little pup," I called out softly. "Where are you, buddy?"

I found the dog cowering under my living room couch, his tiny body trembling with fear. As I approached, he growled, baring his teeth in a defensive posture. I could see the pain and confusion in his eyes, and I knew I had to tread carefully. Poor thing had probably seen Bob die, leaving him traumatized and not knowing what to do without his friend.

"Hey, little guy," I whispered, trying to soothe him. "I know you're scared, but I promise I won't hurt you. We're in this together now, okay?"

The dog's growls subsided slightly, but he still regarded me with suspicion. Slowly, I reached out my hand, giving him the chance to get used to my scent. He did not respond favorably. I considered moving the couch to get to him but thought doing so might make him more scared than leaving him alone.

I filled a small bowl of water, set some bits of chicken left-over from dinner on a saucer, grabbed a throw blanket, and crouched down, placing everything delicately next to the couch. I hoped it all looked enticing enough for the little pooch.

My mind rolled over the trainwreck of a morning I'd just had. Something terrible had apparently happened near my home, a handsome EMT took away my dead neighbor's body by ambulance, and now I had this dog. Bad as it was, it was in keeping with how my life had been going.

I dragged myself to my bedroom, hoping to get another hour or two of sleep before having to face the start of this day a second time.

My room felt especially dark. I tossed in the bed to pull the covers tight around me and lifted my feet to wrap the blankets underneath—a little trick I learned as a child to block the monsters from pulling at my toes. A wind picked up and rattled the windows, reminding me how thin they were. I kicked off the covers, which startled the dog and he started yapping his head off.

The barking followed me as I walked to the living room and grabbed the baseball bat from beside the door. Sliding back under the covers, I laid it on the bed next to me. When I stopped moving, the little chihuahua mix stopped barking. If something sinister was still out there, I doubted Bob's dog could do much to scare it off.

But at least his relentless barking would warn me in enough time to ready the bat.

CHAPTER 2

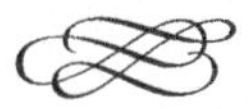

My eyelids were heavy and I could hardly tell if it was still morning or I had slept through the day and it was almost night. The sunlight shining through my blinds from the east indicated I had slept for a couple hours. Albeit fitful ones.

I had tossed and turned, worried about whatever had rattled the EMT, the death of my neighbor, and the tiny, neurotic dog I'd brought into my home.

I heard the dog whining and scratching at the door. "Alright, buddy, I hear you," I muttered, dragging myself out of bed.

I went to the couch where I had left the food and water and saw that the dog hadn't touched the chicken. "What's wrong, buddy? Not hungry?" His animated growl indicated he hadn't grown any weaker for lack of nutrition.

I hoped he had taken a few sips from the water bowl. Maybe he's a vegetarian, I thought. I switched the plate of chicken for one with a dollop of peanut butter. He didn't budge from his spot under the couch. "Dogs like peanut butter," I told him with what I thought was conviction in my voice.

He continued shivering and I gave up for the time being.

I'm nothing before coffee, so I made myself a pot to try to shake off today's first morning.

I stood in a stupor until the coffee finished brewing, then leaned against the counter, sipping the hot, bitter liquid, trying to ignore the pounding in my head. I preferred to drink my coffee black—no sense in adding a cream or sugar barrier to prevent the caffeine from hitting me as fast as possible. I was *this close* to having a power port placed so the caffeine could bypass viscera and go straight to my bloodstream.

After two cups of coffee and twenty minutes of swirling thoughts, I got dressed, grabbed my keys, and headed to the shop. The drive was a short one, under a mile along Point No Point Road. The cool beach breeze coming in through the open car window was a welcome respite from my heavy thoughts, and I breathed in the salty air deeply, attempting to clear my mind.

The employees were already hard at work when I arrived, and I gave them a tired wave.

I went to my small, cluttered office and checked the messages on the ancient landline phone. My cell had been turned off a week ago, and I couldn't afford to turn it back on. Not that cellphones ever worked very well out here in Hansville. As I listened to the messages, which consisted of people asking if their cars were finished yet, I thought about checking the voicemail on my disconnected cell, but I knew it would just be bill collectors. Kenny made sure to apply for lines of credit and set up various utilities under my cell phone number and I didn't need that added stress.

Instead, I push-button dialed my daughter, Bridget. Hers was the only number I had set to memory in the last twenty years. The only other numbers I knew by heart were my parents' landline, which had remained the same for more than forty years—as if they were guarding a sacred relic—and the numbers of a few girlfriends from my childhood, which were likely now useless.

Bridget was the only good thing still remaining from my twenty-two years with Kenny. I'd been seven months pregnant when Kenny and I got married, and he'd raised her as his own from day one. Actually, day one minus eight weeks. He made sure I ate well and took my prenatal vitamins, and was always willing to rub my swollen feet during the last excruciating month of pregnancy. My decision to marry him may have been a nesting instinct. Maybe sometimes, the fastest way to a woman's heart is through her uterus. Maybe that's what it was for me, anyway. But Kenny was kind, he was caring, he was cute as hell, we had been highschool sweethearts, and we loved each other.

"Hey, Bridge," I said when she answered, trying to sound more upbeat than I felt. "Just wanted to check in before you head off to class."

"Hey, Mom," she replied, sounding distracted. Her voice came through the line, barely more clearly than it would have through two tin cans connected by a taut string. "I'm kind of in a rush, but what's up?"

"Not much... I... just checking in. Was thinking about you."

As we spoke, I played with the tangled coils of the cord and traced my finger around the phone to wipe off the dust and grease that had collected between the buttons. Twice, I accidentally pressed one, causing a loud beep that made Bridget think we'd been disconnected.

I talked about the auto repair shop, about the weather, about my plan to have dinner with her grandmother later that night. "Anyways, what did you have for breakfast?" I asked after a long pause, trying to keep her on the line, not wanting to let her go.

She sighed, clearly annoyed by my rambling. "Mom, I've got class. Love you, okay? Bye."

"Bye baby, love you, too," I said, knowing that she'd hung up before hearing my response. I stared at the phone for a moment, feeling an ache in my chest.

Shaking off the lingering hurt, I decided to call my mother, Dorothy. Never far from her phone, she answered after the first ring.

"Hey, Ma," I said, trying to keep my voice steady.

"I was sorry to hear about Bob," she said. "Do you think he will have a memorial? We should throw him a memorial. Don't you think so?"

"I, uhh, maybe." I guess I shouldn't have been surprised that my mother knew Bob had been found dead. She kept track of *everyone* in the area, as though her psychic abilities tracked vital parameters. In truth it was her phone tree—the length of which was matched only by the word count of *Remembrance of Things Past*—that kept her informed of North Kitsap happenings. But even if he didn't have family, wouldn't he have had close relationships with people who would want to be in charge of a memorial? Come to think of it, I didn't know who those friends would be. Likely, most of them had passed away, too.

I was about to ask my mother when she continued, her voice a couple notes lower. "Oh! Did you hear about the girl in Area One?"

"Area One?"

"You know, out near Buck Lake. The state park that borders the Pope Resources land is split up into eight parts. Area One is the section just south of Buck Lake."

Buck Lake was a lovely little spot only about a mile and a half from my house. It was popular for fishing and blackberry picking, and the east side of the lake had a playground and picnic area perfect for birthday parties.

"What happened?" I asked.

"A girl was murdered there last night. Just awful. What kind of a monster would do something so utterly sick?"

"Murdered?" I felt like I was watching myself from outside my body.

"Just a few years younger than Bridget. Cara was her name." Her voice was full of something more than concern.

I felt a lump in my throat. That must have been what Jason was alluding to. "By whom?" The way I asked felt unnatural, but I knew that my mother would correct me if I didn't use 'whom' grammatically.

"They don't know yet," she said. "It's just awful. Bob, and also something like this happening so close to home."

We talked back and forth for a few minutes, and she either didn't know much about how the murder happened or was holding back. I suspected it was the latter. I can always tell when she's keeping something from me. As we spoke, I absentmindedly sifted through the pile of mail on my cluttered desk. A particular envelope caught my attention—it was from the bank. I opened it while still on the phone, and my heart sank as I read the contents.

More debt for The Wrench King—debt my husband had run up to fuel his gambling habit. The rage bubbled up inside me, and I damn near spit on the floor just thinking of him. But spitting on the floor would be a waste of energy. The floor wasn't his eye. And there was no one to clean it up but me.

When talk of the murder began going in circles, I complained to my mom about the debt, but immediately regretted doing so.

My mother, ever the problem-solver, immediately started suggesting ways to handle the situation. "Macy, you should sell the auto repair shop," she said, her voice insistent. "You should—"

"Mom, stop *shoulding* all over my life!" I snapped, cutting her off. "This shop is the only job I have right now. Even if it can't pay down my debt, it's paying for my milk, for God's sake! I can't go back to nursing, at least not yet."

"And no word from that sack of... *ahem...*" my mother cleared her throat. "From Bridget's dad?"

My last job as a nurse was with a home hospice agency in Kitsap County, just across the water from Seattle. Turned out, while I'd been driving from home to home offering comfort-focused care, Kenny had found a way into my computer and was able to intercept Fedex deliveries of narcotics to a number of my patients. So while I'd been wondering what happened to Mr. Smith's Oxycodone prescription, or Mrs. Macgullicutty's Xanax, Kenny had been getting high.

And because it looked like *I* could have been part of the plan to steal the meds—they were my patients, after all—my license had been suspended, pending investigation. The investigation had been stalled for a year because Kenny had fled to Florida and was the only one who could clear my name. Of course, I was let go from my job and couldn't get work as a nurse until further notice. The Wrench King had become my sole source of income and anguish.

I sighed. "I know he's in Florida, but—"

"And he's not sending money? That bas—"

"Bastard, yeah, we agree. But that kind of talk doesn't help me right now, Ma." I didn't need anyone else fueling my fury. I was one strike away from possessing pyrokinesis and the last thing I needed was to burn this place down—*or was it?* "I wouldn't even know how to go about selling the place."

I could hear my mother sigh on the other end of the line, but I pressed on. "Besides, I've learned a lot about cars since he left. I can fix almost anything if I have the right tools and the right YouTube video." I knew I was exaggerating. I was often shooting for the stars. If my wishful thinking got me as high as the moon, who would fault me for my grandiosity?

There was a brief silence.

My *mother*, my mother would fault me for it.

I was relieved when she decided to let it drop—for now at

least—and I steered the conversation back to the horrific event. "Anyway, Ma, tell me more about what you know about the girl, Cara. I know you know more than you're saying."

"I shouldn't say. You have enough on your plate and I don't want you to get all riled up."

"Ma, you're riling me up by *not* telling me."

"Also," she said, "I promised I wouldn't say anything." She paused to give me space to convince her, but I didn't need to because she couldn't hold in the secret any longer. "I heard from Mary who heard from Dennis who heard from CJ that she was strangled. And there was a waxy substance on her neck."

The mention of the waxy substance stopped me cold. I cleared my throat. "Anything else? I mean, what kind of substance? You said 'waxy'?" The last story I'd worked on when I was a crime reporter involved three teenage girls, all of whom were found strangled in a similar fashion.

"Yes, Macy. Like the Waxlace Strangler. But you sent that guy to prison, right?"

"*I* didn't send him anywhere, Ma. I wrote a couple stories on the case. But he was arrested and convicted. They let him out of his psychiatric incarceration about a year ago."

"What do you mean *let him out*? He killed three young girls, Macy. He should be locked up for the rest of his life. They should..."

"Ma," I said, interrupting her 'should' slinging. "They say he'd made progress in managing his mental illness and is no longer a danger to society."

"And you *believe* that? After what he did to those girls?"

"Murderers *do* get let out of prison," I said, trying to keep my voice steady. "And it's not like it was up to *me*." My mother had an odd habit of directing her righteous indignation about the world's shortcomings at whoever she happened to be speaking with. "Believe it or not, Ma, I'm not on the parole board."

"But they've never let a serial killer out before. Have they?"

"Remember John Hinckley Jr.?" I was trying to think of an example from her era. "He shot President Reagan and three others and was released from the psychiatric facility after thirty-five years."

"But he didn't actually *kill* anyone."

"True." I paused, trying to reboot. "There was Herbert Mullin. The Californian who thought he was hearing God. He was killing to prevent earthquakes." When I first heard that the Waxlace Strangler had been let out, I fell down a Google rabbit hole trying to find other examples of serial killers who'd been released. There weren't many, but somehow it made me feel better knowing he wasn't the first.

My mom was incredulous. "Well, they never should have let that guy out, either."

I nodded, then remembered I was on the phone, "Agreed. But, again, not on the parole board, Ma."

"It's just... so horrible."

I took a deep breath. "Have you heard anything else?"

"Not really. After talking to Mary, I texted CJ, and he said he'd call me when he heard more. His brother works with the Kingston Police."

I barely even knew who CJ was, but my mom seemed to have sources in every house in the county. She would have been a great reporter, although I'm not sure she would have been able to consistently separate the spin from the truth.

"Ma," I said, my voice barely a whisper, "did you avoid telling me because you knew I'd worked that case?"

She sighed. "I remembered the articles, Mac. Yeah."

My mother had always been my number one fan. Not only did she know every minutiae of scuttlebut in our tiny town, she knew everything about *me*. She'd kept every bit of childhood artwork and every news article I'd written over the years. I wouldn't be surprised if she kept tissues from a particularly impressive sneeze I'd performed during a childhood sniffle. Unfortunately, she still felt she needed to protect me to a fault.

"And I know it never sat right with you," my mother continued. "You were never sure they got the right guy."

I'd had a few doubts about Jared's guilt, but the evidence that had leaked was pretty convincing. "I try to trust the system. After he was locked up, I never gave it much thought."

That was a lie. Even though I hadn't been a journalist for twenty years, I still thought about the case frequently. I'd reported on it for three months before police arrested Jared Norris, a mentally ill young man who'd later been convicted of brutally strangling the three teenage girls. I'd had a couple good sources and still had my notebooks from the case.

Somewhere.

"Okay," my mother said. "So if you think they got the right guy, and now he's out again. And suddenly another case with a similar... I mean we don't know yet for sure, but a similar... the waxy substance, I mean."

"Out with it, Ma."

"I guess what I'm wondering is, do you think the Waxlace Strangler is back?"

CHAPTER 3

LATER THAT MORNING, I returned home, my mind still reeling from hearing about the murder in the forest near Buck Lake. I suppressed the instinct to call Bridget again after talking with my mother. I knew she'd hear about the murder eventually, but I didn't want her to know any sooner than she had to. Her focus was on school at the moment. And that was where it needed to be.

As I pulled into my driveway, I spotted a man carrying a cardboard box full of papers to a truck parked outside Bob's house. I didn't know for sure whether Bob had children, but this man looked like he could be the right age for that. He was around fifty, with short cropped hair, a tan blazer, and wire-rimmed glasses that made him look like an accountant. In fact, he reminded me of one of the *he-always-seemed-so-normal* types who ends up murdering his wife on those true crime shows I stay up too late watching. Or maybe I was just feeling paranoid.

"Hey," I called out, trying to sound casual. "You related to Bob?"

My smile was met with a flat, disaffected stare.

As I approached, something between surprise and social

anxiety flickered across his face. "Yes." His voice cracked as though he hadn't spoken to anyone in a long time. A *first-conversation-in-the-morning* voice, but it was nearly 10AM. "Name's Bob, too."

"I'm Macy," I replied, extending a hand. "I live next door. I didn't know Bob had a son. I'm sorry about your dad."

He nodded, shifting the weight of the box onto his right forearm and extending his hand from underneath to shake mine. "Thanks, yeah. Bob didn't have any kids. I'm his nephew. We weren't really close, but thanks."

"Oh. Still, I'm sorry."

"I'm... I'm his only living relative, actually." He looked at me nervously.

"So, you're here to settle his estate?" I asked.

"Someone's gotta do it, right?"

I felt a pang of sadness for old Bob, recalling again the way he'd scaled that tree, chainsaw in hand. "You know, I think the only people he really talked to for the last few years were his dog and me." I didn't add the addendum running through my mind: *And we barely talked.*

Nephew Bob's eyes widened. "I didn't know he had a dog." He moved toward the truck and I followed him along the fence.

"I guess you don't know his name then? Little black and white chihuahua mix. Cuter than anything, but meaner, too. Can you take him?"

"No way. I can't take a tiny dog." He heaved up the box and let it drop over the sidewall into the truck bed. "I have two huge dogs at home. They're trained to protect the house. Aggressive, you know. They'd likely crush him by accident. If they decided not to eat him, that is. Dog is better off with you."

For Bob's only living relative, this guy sure didn't seem too concerned with wrapping up his estate compassionately. Felt like he wanted to get things done and get the hell out of there. He started back into the house. "Well, I plan to take him to the pound where they can find him a good home." I sighed, thinking of the little dog's refusal to eat. "You wouldn't happen to know if there's any dog food in the house, would you?"

Nephew Bob shrugged. "I'm not sure, but you're welcome to come in and look."

As I followed him inside, I was struck by the stark contrast between Bob's home and the other beach houses in the area. Having been a reporter and then a nurse, the instinct to notice everything had been deeply instilled in me. So, when looking around Bob's place, I did just that. There wasn't a single seashell, piece of driftwood, or hint of sea glass in sight. The rooms were spotless, but the atmosphere felt cold and sterile. I could almost hear the echoes of loneliness bouncing off the bare, sun-faded, clapboard walls.

Nephew Bob led me towards the center of the home. A golden metal transition strip separated the olive-colored shag carpet of the living room from the formica floor that defined the kitchen. The formica was a staggered pattern of small rectangles in multiple shades of green. The look was dated. Or, *ghastly*, as my mother would say.

I rummaged through the cabinets in search of dog food. I tried to close them lightly, but they were still loud, the felt cabinet bumpers having been worn into oblivion. I searched the kitchen high and low, but there was no dog food to be found.

I chatted away as I searched. "Bob was a good man, I think, but he kept to himself. He must have been through a lot, and he just… closed off from the world." I wondered how different his life might have been if he'd let someone in.

Nephew Bob watched me with either curiosity or suspicion in his eyes. I couldn't tell which.

"So, where are you coming from?" I asked, my journalistic instincts getting the better of me.

"I live in Des Moines."

A sudden wave of worry came over me. It would have taken

a four or five hour flight for Nephew Bob to get here from Des Moines, then a two-hour drive from the airport. Bob had been found only eight hours ago. I was in this kitchen alone, with a man I didn't know, less than half a day after an old man and a young girl were found dead, both less than a mile from my house. I hadn't heard the dog barking its head off. *Could Nephew Bob's truck have come and gone without me hearing it as well?*

I thought about my baseball bat. I thought about buying a gun. Maybe it was time to move from DEFCON Babe Ruth to DEFCON Wild Bill Hickock. Truth was, I couldn't imagine myself wielding a gun. Knowing me, I would definitely pull the trigger, but I probably wouldn't hit what I was aiming at.

"Ohio, huh?" I wasn't proud of it, but I had learned that, as a woman, acting stupid was a tactic I could use to seem less threatening when *I* felt threatened. I kept searching the house, channeling the composure of a poker player.

Nephew Bob cleared his throat. "Iowa, actually. Des Moines is in Iowa."

I glanced over my shoulder at him. At least he was keeping his distance. "Oh, yeah, I remember the limerick: Indiana, Indianapolis, simple and sweet, Iowa, Des Moines is where corn meets concrete."

I was beginning to think that no one had ever owned a dog in this house. Then I saw a small gray dog bed on the far side of the plaid, brown-on-brown, wool-blend couch that made me itchy just looking at it. In contrast to the couch, which was probably from the late sixties or early seventies, the dog bed looked almost new, save for a tiny hole with a bit of puffy stuffing poking out.

I pointed at it. "Do you mind?"

Nephew Bob waved a hand. "Sure, take whatever."

I grabbed the dog bed and made my way out, pausing in the doorway. "Thanks. And, again, sorry about your uncle. He seemed like a good guy."

"Yeah, my mom always said he was." Nephew Bob scratched his head. "She said he was practical, too. I'm thinking he probably just named the thing 'Dog' or something."

It took me a beat to realize he was talking about Bob's dog. "Right, the dog. Oh, like the dog named 'Dog' in *Columbo*?"

Bob looked at me, clearly puzzled. "Is that a movie or something?"

"It's an old show," I mumbled, feeling a bit foolish. "Never mind."

The dog had to have been named either *Dog* or *Bob*, but since it was going to the pound soon, I decided it was best not to assign it a temporary name.

When I walked into my house, the dog was running around manically, growling and barking. The minute I put the little bed down, however, it quieted and settled onto the plush thing as if that's where it belonged. I sighed in relief, then poured myself another cup of coffee and put it in the microwave. Gathering the laundry I'd strewn about on the floor, I started a load in the wash, then searched through an old filing cabinet in the spare bedroom until I found the documents I'd saved from the article I had written about the Waxlace Strangler. It seemed like I should have more papers somewhere.

Quite possibly, I lost them.

I'd never had the best memory, and the chaos of the last few years with Kenny had washed away a good chunk of those I'd been able to retain. It was also possible Kenny had rolled up his tobacco—or God knows what else—in my notes and smoked them.

I took a deep breath to nudge my brain out of the Kenny-shaped hole into which it so often fell.

Throwing on a light jacket, I approached the dog, intending to pick it up off the bed, but the little creature growled and screeched as if in pain. With a sigh, I picked up the entire bed with the dog still on it. The pup instantly fell silent, content in its little nest. I carried the makeshift bundle out the front door and headed for my car, nesting him on the front passenger seat.

Half an hour later we were passing between Poulsbo and Silverdale on State Highway 3. The sun was out and, under normal circumstances, I would have had the cream-colored retractable roof down on my blue VW Cabriolet. But the dog was tiny and I was worried he'd blow away.

As I took the exit for the dog pound, I remembered the coffee I'd left in the microwave. I frowned, a pang of disappointment hitting me.

I could have used that caffeine boost.

THE DOG POUND reeked of disinfectant, a poor attempt at covering the damp fur and animal anxiety smells hanging in the air. The walls were lined with cages, each one holding a lonely, frightened animal. The sounds of barking, yapping, and the occasional whimper echoed through the concrete building, creating a cacophony of despair.

As I approached the reception desk, the tiny dog remained surprisingly calm in its little bed, folded up like a taco. Something stopped me ten feet away from the desk, though. The women there were huddled together and speaking in hushed tones. They were discussing the murder. From the little I could hear, it seemed as though they knew something terrible had happened, but the details were scarce.

I walked away to the edge of the room, reflecting on my day as I waited for their conversation to die down. I had called the local police from the auto shop, only to be informed that the Washington State Patrol had jurisdiction over the case of the strangled girl because the murders happened at a state park.

My plan was to drop off the dog at the pound, then head out

to their office to give them the small pile of papers I'd managed to gather on the Waxlace Strangler. I didn't know whether the cases were connected or not, but passing along the information would make me feel a little better.

Lost in thought, I walked past a room filled with tiny cages, each containing a small, miserable dog. They whined and barked pitifully, their eyes pleading for love and attention. The sight of them made me think of Bob, and that I should have made more of an effort to get to know him. A pang of guilt washed over me. How could I leave this poor creature here, in this place of canine limbo?

I looked up at a poster illustrating what the animal rescue shelters called the "3-3-3 rule." It takes three days for an adopted dog to stop feeling overwhelmed, three weeks to begin to settle in, and three months to build trust and fully bond.

"Ma'am, did you need something?" A woman behind the counter smiled at me sweetly, having looked up from her chat.

"What?" I was lost in thought.

"Can I help you?"

I couldn't do it. I couldn't abandon the dog to this fate. After all, wrapped in its little gray taco bed, the peanut-sized mutt looked cute and friendly. Well, maybe the kind of *cute and friendly* that might turn on you at any moment and chomp off your finger. "Uh, no thank you." I looked down at my dog. "We're just visiting."

I knew the poster referred to how long it takes for a *dog* to go through the stages to feel comfortable in a new home. But as I walked out into the sunshine, I was certain that *I* would be the one experiencing the 3-3-3 rule with my new dog, who was sound asleep in my arms, folded in his taco bed.

Conscience somewhat eased, I hopped back in my car and gently placed the sleeping dog bundle on the front passenger seat. I would give dog ownership a fighting chance. I hoped there would ultimately be less fighting and more affection than there had been up to this point.

I sighed heavily, which seemed to wake him up because he poked his head out of his cocoon and looked around his new surroundings. His attention settled onto me and we stared at each other. His black and white markings reminded me of a dalmatian. A very tiny dalmatian. One with comically short legs and snout, and pointy ears.

"If I am going to keep you, I'll have to figure out how to get you to eat," I warned him. "*And*, I'll need to give you a name."

As I pulled up to the Washington State Patrol office, I felt a mix of anticipation and nervousness.

I wasn't entirely sure what had brought me here. Ever since I was a little girl, I hadn't been able to let anything drop. Whether it was a teacher's unsatisfying explanation about whether trees had personalities when I was four, or my mom's insistence that grunge music would corrupt me when I was thirteen, I had a habit of questioning things until some interior itch got scratched. It made me a good crime reporter, to be sure. And, on my more positive days, I was able to think of myself as *tenacious*. According to Kenny, however, this quality made me "naggy."

The case of the Waxlace Strangler had actually been an exception. I'd worked the story for a Seattle newspaper, and when the case was solved suddenly, I'd let my tenacious self follow it only for a few more weeks. One thing led to another. Work and more work, my first husband disappearing, having a child, moving across the water and marrying Kenny, then trying to keep my head above water during Kenny's downward spiral into debt, gambling, pill-popping, and general ne'er-do-well status.

So maybe it was because that tenacious little girl wanted to resurface after years of lying dormant. Maybe it was because I hated running The Wrench King, and wasn't especially good at it. Or maybe I just needed a change.

But as I walked into the office, carrying the dog under one arm and a stack of papers under another, something in me felt like I was where I was supposed to be.

I approached the receptionist, a kind-looking woman in her late fifties, and she looked up expectantly, waiting for me to state my business. "I might have some information," I told her, "about the case of the strangled girl in the forest near Buck Lake."

She leaned in, her eyes full of concern. "Okay, and what is your name?"

"Macy Ellis. I live—"

"Is this a zoo?" The voice was like a smack to the back of the head. I turned to see a tall, imposing woman approaching from down the hall. Her gray hair was pulled back in a tight bun, her face was set in a permanent frown. She carried herself with an air of authority that demanded respect, and I could tell right away that she was in charge.

"Chief Bangor," the receptionist said. "I'm, I'm sorry. Do you need anything?"

Chief Bangor scowled at me, narrowed her eyes on the dog, then turned back to the receptionist. "I was simply wondering, is this a zoo?"

"What?" The receptionist looked puzzled.

"A zoo!" Chief Bangor repeated.

"No. I. Um..." The receptionist was clearly flustered.

The Chief turned to me. "I need that dog gone." Her voice was cold and cutting.

I fought back a lump in my throat. "I have some information on—"

"Excellent," Chief Bangor interrupted. "I'm sure it will be

case-breakingly important stuff. Please tell us *after* you take the dog out of this building."

I felt a pang of sadness that my new best friend had been dismissed so harshly. But it also solidified my decision to keep him. If this lady—who'd already rubbed me the wrong way—didn't approve of him, the dog was alright by me. Without another word, I headed for the exit.

Upon reaching the parking lot, a glimmer of hope appeared in the form of a man's voice from behind.

"Hey," he called, running after me.

I turned.

He had a strong build—accentuated by a dark brown suit that fit just right—ruggedly handsome features, and piercing brown eyes. His dark hair was cut close but not too close, giving him an air of casual confidence.

"I'm an animal lover too," he said. "If I could, I'd bring my horse with me everywhere."

"I don't think you'd make it very far into that building with a horse."

"I doubt I would," he agreed. "Don't worry about the Chief. She's not all bad. Just not an animal person. My name's Clinton McKenna." He glanced down at the dog. "So, what's your dog's name?" he asked. "And yours too," he added quickly.

"Gonzo," I replied, surprising myself.

"Is that your name or the dog's?" he joked.

"My name's Macy. Macy Ellis, and this is..." I paused, considering my decision... "Yeah, Gonzo."

"Hmm, he looks pretty calm, cool, and collected," Clint observed, a small smile forming on his lips.

"You should see him when he's not asleep. His little nest is round, so he's always waking up on the wrong side of the bed." I chuckled. "He's definitely a Gonzo."

Feeling more at ease, I said, "I might have information on the murder."

Clint raised an eyebrow. “Which murder?”

“The girl.”

He shook his head sadly. “I’m afraid you’ll have to be more specific. WSP has various jurisdictions across the state. We handle a thousand square miles.”

“Sorry, the girl from last night. Strangled. The girl in Area One, out near Buck Lake.”

Clint's expression shifted, his friendly demeanor replaced by a more guarded one.

"I can't talk about that case unless you witnessed something,” he said, his tone cool, almost dismissive. “And I have a court appearance I need to prepare for.”

He turned, but I grabbed his arm. "Did the girl have a strange, waxy substance around her neck?"

Clint turned back to me, his eyes wide. “Nobody’s supposed to know that.”

“But here we are.” I thought of my mother, the scuttlebutt hub of Kitsap County. That woman was always knowing and sharing what she wasn’t supposed to know and share. “Can we talk for a minute?”

He glanced back at the door to the station, then nodded. “I’ll walk you to your car.”

CHAPTER 4

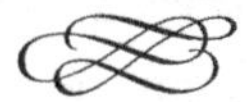

WALKING towards the far side of the parking lot, the warm breeze rustled through the native flora in the parking lot islands. Salal and sword ferns swayed gently, their green hues contrasting with the bright pink blossoms of the Pacific dogwood trees. A faint scent of rosemary wafted through the air, creating an unexpectedly soothing atmosphere in the midst of the dreary asphalt.

Clint's gaze shifted from me to Gonzo, then back to me again. "What do you know?"

"I was a reporter for a bit in Seattle after I graduated from UW. I covered the case of the Waxlace Strangler back in 2001."

As we walked through the parking lot, Clint seemed to be listening intently. "I've heard of the case," he said, "but I don't know any of the details."

We paused near a lush, well-manicured island, and I continued. "The Waxlace Strangler killed three teenagers in 2001. He was arrested and put in a psychiatric prison." I hesitated, realizing that what I was about to say might not be well-received by the law enforcement officer standing before me. "At the time, I had my doubts about whether they got the right guy. After he was arrested, well, I kept following a few leads, then let it go. But I was never sure he was the killer."

Clint raised an eyebrow. "That's a pretty bold claim, Macy. We can't go jumping to conclusions, but it sounds like you know more about this case than I do."

I nodded, understanding his caution, but unable to let go of my gut instinct. "If what I heard about the wax is true, Clint, the similarities... they're hard to ignore."

He sighed, rubbing the back of his neck. A frown creased Clint's brow. "What made you think he could be innocent?"

I shrugged, trying to seem nonchalant despite the gravity of the situation. "I'm not sure exactly, but I have a lot of notes and even a few copies from a police file I got from a source. I thought I had more information, but this is what I found at first glance." I handed him the papers.

He rifled through the stack briefly, then looked up at me. “Thank you for this. These look like they may be helpful.”

“They're all yours,” I said.

“I'll bring them to my office and go through them more carefully.”

“If I find the other papers, I'll bring those in as well.”

“Good. Good,” Clint said.

I realized with a start that I'd almost forgotten I was still holding Gonzo. Cradled in a football clutch under my right arm, he'd been so quiet and still that I worried for a moment he might be dead. But as I looked down at his little, peaceful face, I could see he was content. A small wave of relief washed over me.

I reached down with my left hand and stroked him on the head. To my surprise, he responded by appreciatively licking my fingers. Maybe we would get along after all.

"So, when you were working on this story, did you have any idea about who did it?” Clint asked. “Or did you just think that maybe it wasn't the guy they convicted?"

I nodded, "Yeah, that's right. The latter." My eyes met his briefly. "I don't have any solid proof or anything, but something about the case just never sat right with me. And now, with this new murder... I don't know, all of my thoughts are resurfacing." I took a deep breath. "I can't shake the feeling that the recent murder might be the work of the original killer or a copycat taking advantage of Jared's release."

"Jared? Release?"

"Sorry, Jared Norris, the Waxlace Strangler they called him. The man convicted of the three murders. He was released from psychiatric prison about a year ago."

We fell silent, the enormity of the situation settling over us like a heavy fog.

Clint cleared his throat, breaking the silence with a change in subject. "So, what's your story? You like animals. Are you married? Do you have kids? What news org do you work for now?"

Despite his string of questions, I could tell his mind was still working through what I'd said.

"Woah, *you're* the one sounding like a reporter. I don't work in the media any more. I'm a... a nurse." My voice tripped on the word "nurse" since, technically, I wasn't one anymore, and I was never a good liar. "Or at least, I was. I'm between jobs right now. And married, but separated. I haven't had the chance to finalize the divorce paperwork. One daughter who is grown and out of the house."

Clint eyed me. "You know, we could use someone like you on our WSP special investigations unit. We have a nurse consultant position open."

I hesitated, surprised by his offer. Another thing I'd learned as a woman was that sometimes men offered you jobs because they were too shy to ask you out. "Seriously? What even is a 'nurse consultant'?"

"Specialized role addressing health-related issues within our jurisdiction," he said. "Medical assessments for both victims and suspects, advising on protocols for handling individuals with mental health issues—that's more and more important these days—and training officers on first aid and emergency medical procedures." He paused. "It's part-time, kind of *as-needed.* And you'd need to get your forensic nursing certificate over the next few months. But we're budgeted for a hundred hours a month, market pay."

I looked at him and knew for sure this wasn't an awkward way of hitting on me. Clint didn't have an ounce of sketchiness to him. "I'm not *un*interested," I said, a bit awkwardly. I hoped he knew I was referring to the job, too, not any other sort of relationship.

"Think about it, Macy. Your background in both journalism and nursing could be valuable to us. We'd need to talk to the Chief, but... yeah, this could be good."

One of my favorite things about being a nurse was that any time I didn't like who I was working with—or *for*—or when I grew weary of the type of patient I was seeing, I could switch jobs. I loved the learning aspect of obtaining a new job, and I would certainly learn a lot if I took a job with the Washington State Patrol.

Clint watched me carefully, waiting for a response that I wasn't yet ready to give.

"Can I get back to you on this?" I asked. "I have some stuff to do, and I should probably get going."

"Sure," he said.

I had dinner plans and needed to pick up groceries, but that wasn't what was causing my hesitation. If I wanted this job, and I wasn't sure I did, there was the little issue of my suspended nursing license.

CHAPTER 5

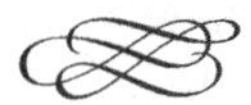

We resumed walking through the parking lot, Gonzo still nestled under my arm. As we stopped at my car, I tapped the retractable roof. "Well, this is me."

Clint's eyes twinkled as he looked at my old, powder-blue Volkswagen Cabriolet. "Interesting choice of car. Originally, the cabriolet was a two-wheeled, one-horse carriage."

I grinned, surprised by the tidbit. "Hmmm... I wasn't aware of its equine origins. This one runs on gas."

"Yes. I figured."

"I call her 'Ice Cream.'"

He raised an eyebrow. "There aren't many blue ice creams."

I leaned against the car, my thoughts drifting back to when I drove it off the lot. "The first week I owned this car, I was at a stoplight and a little girl started yelling, 'ice cream, ice cream!' She ran from her mother out of the crosswalk and kissed one of the headlights, then hugged the front bumper. Hence, 'Ice Cream.'"

A smile tugged at the corner of Clint's mouth. "Sweet."

I was about to unlock the car door when Clint's expression turned serious. "Macy, I wouldn't feel right if I let you go without trying again. The Iron Chief has been on my ass to fill this position. And you know about the nursing shortages. I don't believe in destiny, but I also don't believe in luck. You walked in here today for a reason. Come inside for a bit."

I hesitated, glancing down at Gonzo. He looked up at me with wide, pleading eyes, seemingly aware of the imminent adventure awaiting us. "Okay, but can we go in through the back so no one sees this little guy? I can't just leave him in the car."

"Sure thing," Clint said, and we changed direction, heading towards the back entrance of the station. "There are a few other things I should warn you about if you *do* take the job."

"What's that?" I played along.

"There are only three things in this world I care about: horses, food, and justice. In a perfect world I'm on horseback, eating a poached lobster tail with champagne sauce, riding in the direction of justice, hot on the trail of the bad guys."

I laughed. "Okay, so how'd you end up like that? Strange childhood?"

"That's the other thing you should know. I've got one rule: we don't talk about my past, or my family."

There was clearly a lot more to that story, but I wasn't gonna ignore his only rule on day one.

As we entered Clint's office, I saw it clearly as a reflection of its owner—organized chaos. Stacks of case files and paperwork covered every surface. But every pile was pristinely stacked. I had the feeling that each pile held a purpose only known to Clint. He gestured for me to sit in a worn leather chair across from his oak desk and I obliged, clutching Gonzo protectively in my lap.

He fired up his laptop and began typing. "Jared Norris you said?"

I nodded. "Yup."

As he typed, his brow furrowed. "So, I've got some news for

you. According to this, Jared has been living alone since his release, on probation with strict curfew parameters."

My stomach tightened. "You think he could be connected to the recent murder?"

"I'm not there yet," Clint replied. He scanned his computer screen. "But you are right, there are similarities we can't ignore."

I looked around the office, taking in the organized mess, and thought about how out of place I felt. Clint's gaze met mine and he offered a warm smile. "Macy, take the job. At first, you'd be shadowing with me, while we wait for your background check and nursing license verification. But you really could do some good."

I bit my lip, unwilling to share the truth about my suspension. "I'll think about it, Clint."

"Would you like to know more details about the case?" He leaned back in his chair, holding up a stack of what appeared to be crime scene photos. "Might help you make up your mind. I shouldn't be sharing these with you but, I will on occasion break the rules if I think doing so will help us catch a murderer."

My journalist instinct kicked in, and I agreed to take a look at the pictures he was handing me.

The first picture showed the body of the girl on the damp ground, half covered in clumps of moss and wet leaves. Dew clung to her hair and her neck was bruised and swollen from the strangulation. Her eyes were open, staring at something too distant for living eyes to see. It was gruesome.

The next picture showed a closeup of her shirt, which had been torn near the shoulder.

Clint's voice took on a somber tone. "No evidence of rape," he said, shaking his head. "But this is one of the most brutal crimes I've seen."

I had no words. The photos were chilling, very similar to the ones I'd looked at all those years ago.

"Sickening," Clint continued. "The wickedness people are

capable of." The way he said it was like he was sharing a dark secret we were both privy to.

My heart ached for the girl's mother. I thought about Bridget, now in her second year of nursing school at Olympic Community College.

Clint's eyes searched mine for a reaction.

I shook my head. "I don't know, Clint. These pictures make it look like it could be the same killer. But look, it could also be someone else. What do *I* know? I can't sign onto the case, but if I think of anything else that could help, or find those other papers, I'll let you know."

He seemed disappointed, but handed me his card. "In case you change your mind."

I took the card, tucking it into my pocket, my thoughts racing. We sat in silence for a moment, the weight of the gruesome photos hanging heavy between us. "Is there anything else you need from me?" I asked, my voice quiet.

"No, not right now," Clint answered. "But remember, if you change your mind, I'm here." His eyes locked on mine and, for a moment, I felt as though he wanted me to save him from the nightmare of this case.

I nodded. "Thanks, Clint. I appreciate it."

I tore my gaze from him and let myself and Gonzo out.

CHAPTER 6

THE VIEW from my mother's dining room was always soothing.

Through the large windows, the waters of the Puget Sound were calm and serene, reflecting the bright, late-afternoon sun. The shoreline was bursting with the bright greenery of the last vestiges of summer. Soon a deeper green would set in as the fall brought even more rain.

As I took my seat at the dining table next to Grandma Ethel, I asked, "Where's Pa?"

"He's up in his lair," my mother replied, placing lumpia on the table.

My father had a giant workshop on the back of the property where he spent most of his time. He returned to the main house only to sleep and eat. He preferred to interact with other humans only long enough to sustain life.

Grandma Ethel reached out to the plate, touching nearly every lumpia on the platter before selecting one. At nearly a hundred years old, she was afforded some liberties not granted to the rest of us.

“Salmon will be ready soon,” my mother said. “But we can start with these. I know they’re your favorite.”

I grabbed a hot, crispy lumpia off the plate. "They smell amazing."

"Rosamie was over last week and we made a six-month supply, which should last us two months. I'll send some home with you."

Rosamie and my mother had worked together for over three decades in a nursing home in Poulsbo. They could not get enough time together. When I was young, my mother would come home late from a shift and be on the phone with her within the first few minutes of walking in the door. They would go on endlessly about their patients and how best to care for them or rehash some crazy thing a patient had done that day. I would be halfway through my dinner before my mother sat down to the now lukewarm meal she had set out for herself.

As I dug into the lumpia, my mother sat across from me. "So, did you hear anything more about the..." she lowered her voice... "the murder?"

It was times like these that Grandma Ethel's near deaf state came in handy. Ethel did not need to hear about the brutal strangling of a young girl. Not in what all the doctors were saying were the last few months of her life.

But Grandma Ethel had been in "the last few months of her life" for the past eight years. Perhaps her near deafness shielded her from information that would otherwise send her to an early grave. Well, not early, relatively speaking.

Just as I was about to reach for another lumpia, Gonzo jumped onto a chair and then onto the table. He sat in front of my plate, whining for food.

Grandma Ethel looked up. "Shoo, shoo," she said weakly, flapping her hand in the direction of Gonzo.

Gonzo glared at her, then realizing she was no threat, turned back towards me with pleading eyes.

"Do you think Bob fed him like this?" I asked. "He wouldn't eat from the bowl I set down earlier."

I hand fed Gonzo a corner of a lumpia. He ate it eagerly, but gently. Through his piranha-like insatiability, he somehow maintained a respect for the tips of my fingers, making a soft *mmmm... mmm...* noise while he ate. Likely the cutest sound Grandma Ethel had not heard in her life.

My mother frowned. "Macy, that's disgusting."

"Mom, this dog has been through a lot recently," I insisted, feeding him bite after bite. "Cut him some slack."

She sighed and fetched a small bowl of water for Gonzo, who lapped it up gratefully before hopping back down and scampering to his bed. I knew he shouldn't live on lumpia alone any more than I should, but at that moment I couldn't force myself to deprive either of us.

Next, my mother brought in and served the salmon. She had layered thin slices of lemon on the fish, then used the barbeque to cook each piece on an individual cedar plank. I wished I hadn't eaten so much lumpia, but I could never resist.

While we ate, the conversation about the murder of the young girl continued. "I think you went to school with her mom," my mother said. "Do you remember a Nancy? Nancy McDonald, maybe?"

"I don't recall. Maybe if I saw a picture. I can't imagine what she must be going through. That poor mother."

There was a pause and I imagined my mother was thinking about Bridget too.

"Did I tell you what is on sale at Costco?" my mother suddenly blurted out.

I raised an eyebrow. "Really, Ma? *Costco*?"

If my grandmother could prolong her life by using her deafness to evade reality, my mother could do the same by distracting herself with the latest sale at Costco. And there was *always* a sale at Costco. My mother was going to live forever, too.

"Well, they have great deals right now," she insisted, her

voice filled with forced excitement, "paper towels and frozen shrimp."

I felt mildly irritated. "Let's not talk about Costco, Mom."

"Heard from..." she cleared her throat, knowing she shouldn't finish the sentence, but unable to stop herself, "...from *Bruce?*"

Bruce was Bridget's biological father. He was also my first husband, not to mention a *missing person*. We'd gotten married when I was twenty, a junior at UW. At twenty-five, he'd been an up-and-coming TV news man at KOMO 4 News in Seattle. He was handsome, smart, and made me feel like I could be anything, do anything.

I'd gotten pregnant toward the end of my senior year and, despite the fact that it was unplanned, I was thrilled. So was Bruce. At least that's what I thought. Bruce was making good money by that point, so our plan was that I would take a couple years off to stay at home, then get right back into crime reporting.

Then—around Christmas of 2001—he disappeared. And not like *ran-off-with-a-cocktail-waitress* disappeared. He disappeared from the face of the earth. Left me, left his job, left his friends. Left $10,000 in cash on the kitchen table, packed a suitcase, and left. No note.

I scoured the internet, even hired a private investigator. I still remember meeting the guy I hired, who refused to charge me because I was broke and pregnant and he hadn't found a damn thing. Shaking his head sadly, he'd concluded: "Either Bruce Wade is a fake name, a fake persona, or he was a figment of your imagination." I hadn't heard a word from him ever since. The only proof I had of his existence was what he had left growing in my belly. And I was far from being an immaculate conception.

Ranking just behind Costco, Bruce was my mother's go-to topic when faced with difficulty or a lull in the conversation.

I scowled. "No, Ma. I promise, you'll be the first person I tell if and when he magically reappears."

A tense silence fell over the room, and I knew my mother's thoughts were mirroring my own. We both wanted to escape the pain and fear that came with discussing the murder. But her evasive tactics only reminded me how much the situation affected us all.

After a long silence, I changed the subject. "They offered me a job with the Washington State Patrol."

"Really?" my mother asked.

"They have a nurse consultant position open."

"Macy, you *need* a job. You should take the position."

"I can't," I sighed. My stomach was bloated with lumpia, and I could only poke my fork at the half-eaten piece of salmon. "Remember. My nursing license… Kenny…."

"Oh, *him*," she scoffed, her face contorting with disdain. "I can't believe you ever married that man." She didn't even like saying his name.

"It seemed like a good idea at the time," I said.

"I'm just surprised it was pill-thieving that eventually ended your marriage, rather than his various doomed investments."

We couldn't help but laugh. Since Kenny had left for Florida, it was either laugh at the situation, or never stop crying.

"What are you two going on laughing about?" Grandma Ethel asked, trying to join the conversation.

My mother looked straight at her and spoke slowly so Ethel could read her lips. "We're talking about Macy's soon-to-be ex husband."

"Oh," Ethel responded dispassionately. Sometimes it was hard to tell if grandma genuinely understood us or was placating to conceal the extent of her hearing loss. There was a long pause, but I could tell she had more to say because of the way she held a single bony finger in the air. "I have the mind to make that boy go pick out a *switch*," she said at last, waving her fork for emphasis. She continued eating, fighting her tremor so the food on her fork would reach her mouth.

She *had* heard us.

"Ugh, grandma," I said, shaking my head. She'd gone back to eating, and I knew she wouldn't be able to hear me through her own chewing. I said to my mom, "She's probably thinking about the time he tried to sell her on that pyramid scheme."

My mother snorted. "Oh, please. As if we need more overpriced, useless products cluttering our house."

"We get enough of those from Costco," I jabbed.

"Costco is *not* overpriced, Mac," my mother said, defensively.

"You're right mom, we should *definitely* spend more time talking over the specifics of prices at Costco."

"Hey, you brought up Costco this time," my mother pointed out.

"I wonder who taught me *that*?"

We both burst into laughter, but I knew that she was just as aware as I was about the topic we were avoiding.

"Listen, Macy," my mother said, "they won't find out about your suspended license if you don't tell them. At least not right away."

I cocked my head to the side, waiting for her to look at me. "So, you suggest I lie to the police?"

"Police lie all the time."

"Ma, police are *allowed* to lie to the public. It's the public that isn't allowed to lie to the police."

"Well," she retorted, a playful glint in her eye, "if you're *working* for the police, that means you can lie, too."

"I'm certain that's not how it works Ma."

"Still, you should take the job."

"Oh, *should* I?" My mother knew this was the point where I would bail on the conversation. I always cut her off when she started *shoulding*.

I considered her words, but doubted I could bring myself to

take the job under false pretenses. I shook my head. "No, Ma. I can't do it."

She sighed, relenting. "Fine, but just think about it, okay?"

The conversation left me feeling emotionally drained. Between the 3 AM sirens outside my house, the death of my neighbor, the murder at Buck Lake, and the recent addition of a neurotic chihuahua that doubled my current family unit, I desperately needed a break.

I bussed our plates to the sink as my mother plated food for my father and delicately covered it with transparent film. She would reheat the meal when he returned from his lair.

I said goodbye and headed for the car.

Today, life had thrown me one curveball after another and I needed simple comforts more than anything else. I was stuffed, but later that night I would likely still eat all the lumpia my mother had packed up for me. All I wanted was to curl up in front of the television with a quilt crocheted by my grandmother, a red beer, and a rerun of *Murder, She Wrote.*

I just wanted to lose myself in someone else's mystery. One that I wasn't responsible for solving.

CHAPTER 7

THE SUN WAS BARELY UP when I walked into the auto repair shop's cramped little office, greeted by the familiar perfume of grease and oil mixed with stale coffee and lingering exhaust fumes. Gonzo settled into his makeshift bed on the corner of my desk, nursing a food coma after gorging on last night's left-over salmon for breakfast.

I swear he'd consumed half his body weight in fish.

As I surveyed the growing mountain of unopened mail on my desk, I muttered, "I really don't want to deal with any more bad news."

"What's that, boss?" Iggy, my gruff, oil-stained mechanic had caught me talking to myself. He was a tall man with a scruffy beard and a bald head that always seemed to sport a greasy smudge. His muscular arms were covered in tattoos, a roadmap of his life's passions and mistakes.

"Nothing, Iggy," I replied, waving him off. "Just thinking out loud. You think there's anything good in that pile of mail?"

"What?" he asked, wiping his hands on a grease-stained rag.

The cacophony of the shop had drowned out my voice.

"Never mind," I sighed, deciding that even if something good was buried in that stack, I wasn't ready to face the onslaught of bad news to find it.

I plopped down in my chair and started up the computer, which was one generation newer than dial-up. I opened up the bookkeeping software Kenny had installed but never used, then scrolled over to Facebook. If I was looking for distraction from the debt threatening to wash the autobody shop into the Puget Sound or the murder that had given me nightmares, I'd gone to the wrong place.

The first thing I saw was a post from Nancy McDonald, the mother of Cara, the girl who'd been found dead.

Please, I'm begging you, if anyone knows anything or can do anything to help us find out what happened to our baby girl, we need your help. We're lost without her, and we need justice. I can't bear this pain any longer. 💔😢

I clicked on the profile picture of the woman, who looked vaguely familiar. Light brown hair, blue eyes, and a round face that looked pleasant and happy. I'd definitely gone to school with her. How else would we have become Facebook friends?

My heart ached. This mother's grief-stricken words stirred something inside me.

It's strange. I'd watched a hundred shows about murder, read a hundred articles, even written a few dozen myself. I'd watched documentaries about the most gruesome crimes imaginable and still kept an emotional distance. I'm not sure why, but staring at that Facebook post as the sounds and smells of the autobody shop spilled in from all sides, I couldn't keep my distance anymore. Cara's death hit me hard. It could just as easily have been Bridget.

I *had* to do something.

I quickly pulled up the International Association of Forensic Nurses' website, and the words on the screen drew me in immediately. I devoured the information. Scrolling through the requirements to become a certified forensic nurse, I felt a spark

I hadn't felt in years. Clint had mentioned that he could take me on on a preliminary basis as I earned a forensic nursing certificate. But that was something I could acquire during the first few months of employment.

"Gonzo! I'm gonna do it."

The little thing stirred in his bed, clearly annoyed at being disturbed from his slumber. I gave him a pat on the head and he returned the gesture with frenetic licking. He didn't just let me pet him, he was compelled to immediately return the affection via tiny tongue lashings. For better or worse, he did nothing half hearted.

I turned my attention back to the website.

My background seemed like a perfect fit for this new career path. My years as a crime reporter had honed my investigative skills and my time spent as an ER and psychiatric nurse had given me hands-on experience in high-pressure situations. The sensitivity I'd developed as a hospice nurse would surely be an asset dealing with traumatized victims. And, of course, my love of *Murder, She Wrote* reruns and true crime documentaries didn't hurt either.

I signed up for a membership and enrolled in a continuing education class on addressing intimate partner violence. As I read through pages of text and clicked through worksheets, I felt grateful that, despite all of Kenny's many shortcomings, I'd never had to worry about him hurting me or Bridget physically. A low bar, to be sure, but still it was a higher one than some people had.

The financial mess he'd left behind was another story, but I decided to use that as fuel to propel me forward. I knew I'd have to be discreet about my suspended nursing license, but I justified it by thinking of the good I could do, the lives I could potentially improve.

I picked up my old landline and dialed. "Hey, Clint, where do I sign up?"

There was a brief pause on the other end before he answered. "Oh, huh? Is this Macy, Macy Ellis?"

"Yeah, but you can call me Mac."

"So, you want to join the force after all?"

"That's the plan," I said, verbally reinforcing my own decision.

"Come on down to the station today. We'll start the paperwork."

"Today?"

"How soon can you get here? We're getting new information about the murder, and I just received more files on the Waxlace Strangler. Some of it you might already know, some… well… it might help for you to take a look."

"I'll be there in an hour and a half," I replied. My heart was racing.

As I hung up the phone, I glanced down at my outfit. My shirt was stained with motor oil, my jeans were stained with coffee, motor oil, and God knew what else. I could see unshaved knee hair through unintentional pant leg holes. This was definitely not the attire I should be wearing for my first meeting with my new boss.

CHAPTER 8

Back at home, I dug into the back of my bedroom closet and pulled out my trusty interview costume: black slacks, a white shirt with an oversized collar, and a faded blue blazer. The outfit let the world know, *I'm a professional woman, buuuuut I'm kinda broke right now.* It had been quite some time since I'd needed to dress up.

It was the same number I'd worn for my last job interview five years ago, and it would have to work its magic again today.

I broke out the iron from a shelf that required the use of my step stool to reach. I had to make these clothes look halfway decent. These days, most of my nicest articles of clothing were scrubs. But those wouldn't be appropriate for shadowing Clint any more than the tatters I was wearing at the moment would.

I inspected the iron and covered a section of its frayed cord with electrical tape before plugging it in. It was my grandmother's, built in an era when electrical cords were insulated with flammable materials, no longer legal in the United States.

I sustained a small burn on my fingertip testing the iron for readiness. But I counted not electrocuting myself as a major win.

I was unpracticed and had to iron out more creases I inadvertently made than were present on the outfit in the first place. I was like that poor slug from the math problem, the one that climbed two inches up the flagpole every day, only to slide back down an inch every night. I never got that math problem right the first time. I was too concerned about the slug's plight to concentrate. Depressing, isn't it, that even the efforts of a slug are subject to entropy?

When the outfit looked halfway decent, I dressed, then hurried off to my parent's house, where I left Gonzo with my mother before speeding out to the station.

As I approached the entrance, I plucked tiny white and black hairs off my blazer. I felt the negative space under my arm where Gonzo had been for the last day. Damn. I'd already become codependent with the little animal. From the way his hairs clung to everything, it looked like, even when I left him, I would never be totally without his presence.

While crossing the parking lot, a man I didn't recognize made a beeline for me. He was tall, with dark hair and eyes that held a mischievous glint. He had the kind of smile that made you feel like you were in on a secret, even if you had no idea what it was. Despite my irritation at his unsolicited approach, I had to admit he was handsome.

"Excuse me, are you Macy Ellis?" he asked, extending his hand.

I hesitated for a moment before shaking it. "That's me. And you are?"

"Brian Schmidt, local reporter." As he spoke, his smile never wavered. "I heard you're involved in the Area One murder case. Do you have any comments?"

I considered this. I accepted the job only ninety minutes ago and the only person I'd told was my mother. Oh, right, my *mother*. "Lemme guess," I said. "You know Dorothy Ellis? Or someone who knows her?"

Brian smiled. “My mom plays cards with her.”

I sighed, trying to maintain my composure. "No comment, Brian." My mother had probably told Brian’s mother I was single, too. Fortunately, she hadn’t shared the news about my suspended nursing license. If she had, Brian would have brought it up immediately.

His eyebrow jerked up, his smile widening. "Come on, Macy. I did my research. I've read your articles. You used to be one of us. You know how this works."

I looked at him, remembering the constant pressure to get a scoop, the adrenaline rush of chasing a story. "Yeah, I know how it works," I said, a hint of a smile playing on my lips despite my best efforts to withhold it. "But I also know when to back off.”

“This is no time for me to back off.”

“No *comment*, Brian," I said.

He leaned in, his voice conspiratorial. "You know, I don't give up that easily. I've got a nose for news."

I crossed my arms and smirked. "Well, I've got a mind for helping the police. Let's see who comes out on top."

He laughed, clearly amused. "I like your spirit, Macy."

As I brushed past him, I felt a twinge of satisfaction that I'd dressed up. I was forty-four years old, single, and swimming in debt. If I had any shot with a guy like Brian, at least I didn't look like I'd just crawled out from under a car. I pushed the thought aside, reminding myself that I had more important things to focus on. My constant random crushes were going to get me into trouble if I didn’t get a hold of myself. At some point I would have to start dating again, but right now I had no time for dalliances.

I stepped into the state patrol office, trying to shake off the encounter.

As I walked down the hallway, a peculiar poster on the wall grabbed my attention. A dog dressed as a police officer stood proudly, handcuffing a sly-looking cat. The caption read: "We’ll sniff out the lie, so don't even try." The poster was both amusing and unsettling, considering I'd been less than honest about my suspended nursing license.

Before I could finish admonishing myself, I spotted Jacqueline—*The Iron Chief,* as Clint had called her—walking alongside Clint. She looked me up and down, her eyebrows raised, and said, "Well, at least you didn't bring the dog this time."

I forced a smile and replied, "Gonzo's with my mother. I figured this wasn't a 'bring your dog to work' kind of day."

Jacqueline's lips curled into a smirk as she walked away. Turning to Clint, I gestured to the poster and said, "You know, with a poster like that, you'd think they'd be more open to having animals around here."

Clint chuckled, "I had that put up last year. Maybe what we need is a few *more* animal posters around here. I should get one with a horse on it." He turned to me and stopped, making his voice hokey and exaggerated, like a radio advertisement from the fifties. "In the pursuit of justice, *neigh-ver* give up!"

I offered up a charity laugh and let Clint guide me into a small, cramped conference room. The whiteboard on the wall had seen better days, and the worn particle-board table in the center of the room sagged slightly in the middle. I imagined the years of paperwork and cups full of stale coffee overburdening the counterfeit wood top. The room smelled stale, a mix of coffee sweetened with international delight and sweat lingering on cotton-blend polyester. It was far from cozy, but it was clear that serious work happened within these walls.

As Clint took his seat in front of the whiteboard, the door burst open and two detectives entered. They were tall, athletic, and well-dressed, with sharp features and dark hair that framed their faces. They looked to be in their mid-to-late thirties. The striking resemblance between the two was uncanny.

"Ah, perfect timing," Clint said, motioning to the newcomers.

"Macy, meet Carlo and Maria. They'll be working with us on the case."

I tried to keep my surprise in check as I extended my hand to each of them in turn. "Nice to meet you both. I'm Macy."

Carlo shook my hand firmly, his grip strong and confident. "Welcome aboard. Clint told us he hoped you would be joining. We're glad to have you on the team."

Maria followed suit, her handshake equally firm. "Clint has told us good things about you. It'll be great to work together."

I tried to ignore my gnawing curiosity about Carlo and Maria. Were they twins? Twins or not, they might know something about Clint's past and why he didn't talk about it.

I warned myself not to turn into my mother. But, there were a few burning questions I was itching to ask behind my held tongue.

CHAPTER 9

AT THE FRONT of the room, Clint prepared for the meeting, going over notes and organizing files. Carlo and Maria found their seats at the table and sat next to each other.

As I studied them, Carlo reached behind Maria's ear. She looked at him quizzically. "Are you doing that magic penny trick on me? Knock it off." She batted her hands at him playfully.

Carlo shook his head, smirking. "No, there's actually something in your hair." He pulled a candy wrapper out from behind her ear.

Maria laughed. "Give me that. I don't even *eat* candy."

"*Suuuure* you don't," Carlo said. He stood and altered his voice, making it commanding a little grating. "I need that candy *gone*. What is this, a *candy* shop?"

"You do a good Iron Chief," I said. "What is her deal? She doesn't like candy? What's her thing about not liking animals?"

"Anything that might distract us from making her look good to the higher ups is out," Maria warned. "And animals…"

"Traumatic experience," Carlo said, less of an interruption, more a continuation of Maria's thought. "A horse rolled over on her during a competition. There's a YouTube video of it. The thing just sat down mid course and rolled onto its back. After that, she never got back in the saddle." He stood up and tossed the wrapper into a nearby trash bin.

"Two points!" Maria cheered.

She and Carlo exchanged a high five as Carlo sat down next to her.

"Will you two knock it off?" Clint interjected. "One of these days you'll be in a situation and need professionalism. I swear the two of you won't have the capacity to keep things serious."

Even though they looked like they could be siblings, Carlo and Maria seemed to be flirting. It was hard to tell, and I no longer had much trust in my instincts around the art of the flirt. My mind had decided these two would take up the same neuronal pathways as the brother and sister from a long time ago in a galaxy far, far away. I made a mental note to never accidentally call them Luke and Leia out loud, and another one to ask Clint about their relationship later. Even if it turned me into my mother, I had to know.

Under Clint's guidance, we gathered around the worn table to discuss the case. Clint took the lead, laying out the plan. "Macy and I will interview Nancy McDonald, the mother of the deceased girl, Cara. She lives in Poulsbo. From there we're going to head to Seattle to question Jared, the man convicted previously as the Waxlace Strangler. Maybe we'll get lucky and he'll admit his guilt. Maria, Carlo, you two head back to the crime scene to meet with the crime scene unit for updates."

He paused, studying the whiteboard, then turning back to us. "Any questions?" he asked. "Anything to add?"

"I have something," I began. "It doesn't exactly make sense that this could be connected, but I feel it's something I should bring up."

"Go ahead," Clint encouraged.

"The night of the murder, my neighbor Bob was found dead. Natural causes, they said. Which makes sense because the guy was in his nineties. But, the thing is, the very next day his nephew was there taking care of his estate. Something about him felt a little off."

"As in, *just-killed-his-uncle* off?" Carlo asked.

"What person isn't a bit off?" Maria countered. "Especially if they are dealing with their dead uncle's belongings."

"Macy, you're a nurse," Clint said. "Could they have misclassified Bob's cause of death?"

"I don't know," I answered. "A week earlier he was up a tree in my yard with a chainsaw. Seemed like he had a lot of life left in him."

"Did the uncle have money?" Carlo asked.

I'd never seen any evidence he was wealthy, and the interior of his house definitely hadn't been updated this century. "I don't know about any money. His tiny house would be worth a pretty penny. Right on the beach and all. I mean, if he didn't have a reverse mortgage or other debts."

"Something to look into," Clint said.

"The thing that's strange," I said, "is that Bob's nephew said he came from Iowa. And I don't see how he could have made it from Iowa to Hansville in that time frame." I scanned the faces of my new teammates and shrugged.

"We'd have to put together a timeline. Get his travel plans," Clint added, nodding at Maria. "Get on that?"

She jotted a note on a small pad. "On it. A potential double homicide then?" Maria asked.

"We don't know anything yet," Clint said, "let's just start gathering the information."

Our conversation was interrupted by a young man entering the conference room and handing Clint a manila file. He looked no older than twenty. "The delivery agent said you'd want these right away, Captain." His voice was disorientingly deep and delivered with a thick vocal fry.

"Thanks, Eddie," Clint said as he opened the file. He gave a throaty cough as though that would clear the irritation we all imagined *Eddie's* vocal cords were suffering from.

Quietly, he flipped through a few of the pages. "This is a partial set of the files from the Waxlace Strangler case. Macy, you might be familiar with some of it."

Maria said, "I think I was a senior in high school when this went down."

"Same," Carlo said.

Clint began placing photographs down on the desk in front of us.

Though I'd seen some of them before, others were new to me. One of the photographs was an image of Jared Norris, apparently taken from the days after his arrest. In it, he looked like no more than a gangly teenager. He showed no obvious defensive marks on his arms and hands, no scratches on his face, nothing.

"Hey, everyone," I said, my voice wavering a bit. "This was taken a few days after the third strangling. I'm not sure about this, but take a look. Jared doesn't have any defensive marks on him. No scratches, no bruises. You see his hands, no marks, but they found Jared's blood on the shoelace. The prosecution said the blood was from Jared using his hands on the laces to strangle the girls. Wouldn't there have been marks on his hands?"

Carlo leaned in, his brow furrowed as he studied the image. "Could have worn gloves."

Maria chimed in, her tone thoughtful. "Maybe the blood wasn't from his hands. Either way, it was *his* blood, right? DNA came through?"

Clint nodded, holding up a stack of papers. "DNA was a 99.99% match. Jared's blood was on the shoelaces used to strangle the girls."

"The third girl," I corrected. "They never found any direct evidence tying him to the first two."

"Right," Carlo said, "but since the MO was the same…"

"They nailed him for all three," Maria concluded.

In another photo, a closeup of one of the victims' necks, I saw the familiar waxy substance. "The wax was found on all the victims," I said.

"And it's on the new victim as well," Clint added. "Nearly identical."

In Jared's trial, prosecution had shown that the wax was from shoelaces, the extra-thick kinds worn by hockey players. Jared had worked at a Seattle ice-skating rink.

Clint said, "Jared has already been questioned by law enforcement in Seattle. He *seems* to have an alibi for the night of the recent murder. But everyone who interviewed him has this sinking feeling that he's still somehow involved in the killings then and now. Officer I spoke with this morning said Jared's either our killer or he's the craziest non-killer he's ever met." Clint shook his head. "Anyway, Jared's blaming some guy named Heath for the original murders, as well as this recent one."

"Any last name?" Maria asked, jotting notes.

I crossed my arms, feeling uneasy. "I don't remember any 'Heath' from the original case."

Clint shook his head. "Sounds like Jared may have invented him."

"Where is Jared now?" I asked.

"Seattle," Clint said. "Being watched closely, so we don't have to worry about him fleeing. We can go question him as soon as we're ready."

We went back and forth, considering the possibilities. It could be a copycat killer, or maybe just a coincidence. The murders were twenty years apart and took place in entirely different locations, so they weren't exactly identical.

As we mulled over the facts, a sense of urgency crept into my thoughts. I recalled the timeline of the original murders, and suddenly, a disturbing thought sprang to mind. "What if this killer is on a schedule?" I asked, my voice unsteady. "The original murders happened one week apart, right? So, if this is the same person, we have exactly one week to save the next potential victim."

The room grew tense as the weight of my words sunk in. Everyone exchanged glances, and Clint nodded in agreement. "Like I said, we don't know anything yet, except that we can't afford to waste any time."

Carlo chimed in, his voice a mix of determination and uncertainty. "We'll look into Macy's Bob character and then head over to the crime scene."

"Right, Carlo," Clint said. "Macy and I will head over to speak with the girl's mother, then track down Jared for questioning."

CHAPTER 10

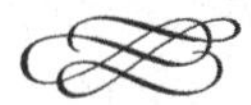

"HEY, can I use your phone to check my voicemail?" I asked Clint as he steered us toward Poulsbo, toward the apartment of the victim's mother. "Mine's not working."

He nodded toward the center console and I picked up the phone. Thankfully, his reply was without probing questions. Technically I hadn't *lied*. My phone was, in fact, not working. Clint didn't need to know that it had been shut off due to lack of payment.

The robotic voice on the other end of the line greeted me with a monotone, "You have forty-three messages..." That was a level of hell I was not prepared for today, especially in front of my new boss. The first was a message from Kenny from a week earlier, the night after my phone had been turned off. It started with, "Did you get the money I sent?"

"Yeah, right," I whispered under my breath, hanging up immediately. Kenny often used a compliment or promise of money to get me to hear him out before springing the real message on me—usually a request for a favor, or, worse, a request to get back together with him.

"What's that?" Clint asked, catching my mutterings.

"Nothing important," I replied, returning the phone to the center console. I could deal with the other forty-two messages later. I'd reached my daily threshold of doing things to try to turn my life around. At this rate, I would still be up to my neck in chaos by the time I took to my deathbed.

We pulled up to the apartment building and spotted a group of reporters, including Brian Schmidt, the handsome yet annoying man who'd greeted me outside the offices of the Washington State Patrol. As we walked past them, Clint and I both offered only curt *no comments.*

Then we saw the horse.

The small, stocky quarter horse swatted flies with its patchy tail, shuffling along the parking lot like it was out in a lovely field. Her scuffed hooves and worn shoes clopped with each ambling step of her stubby legs, wobbling under an ungroomed chestnut coat dappled with gray.

I couldn't help but laugh. "Are you kidding me?"

Clint approached an old guy in a white bathrobe, who was sitting on a folding chair out front of the apartment complex, scratching himself as though the parking lot were his private living room.

"Do you know whose horse this is?" Clint asked.

"Yeah, that's the Smith's horse," the man replied nonchalantly. "They live on the third floor."

The horse began licking the ground. The reporters didn't seem the least bit interested in the free-range urban horse. As the saying goes in reporting, *If it bleeds, it leads.* They were here hoping to grab a morsel of content from the strangled girl's mother.

"Is this where they board their horse?" Clint asked the neighbor, who was mid-scratch.

"They board him at a stable just up the hill and ride him after school. He comes down here every few days when he can break out of the paddock. He knows there's spilled soda on the ground at the kid's bus stop down here. It's like he can smell it."

"Shouldn't we catch him?" I asked.

"We *should* catch him," Clint agreed. "We don't want it to cause a car accident."

"Well, you'll need some soda," the bathrobed neighbor said, flashing a gap-toothed smile. He was loving every second of this.

"I'll catch him," Clint said, ignoring the neighbor's recommendation.

I raised an eyebrow. "Okay, Mr. Horse Whisperer."

"I got this," he said, striding forward. As Clint approached the horse, it stepped to the side, evading him as though it had eyes in the back of its head. Next, Clint attempted to approach the horse from three different angles. But each time it neighed and bolted a few strides away, then continued licking the ground.

The bathrobed neighbor laughed like he was three beers in at a comedy club. "I told you, you'll need a soda." As Clint tried again, the neighbor ambled into his apartment, then returned with a can of root beer and a long orange extension cord. At the sound of the can being opened, the horse perked his ears back and walked toward the neighbor calmly.

By now, half of the reporters had shifted their attention from the door of the apartment building to the scene unfolding before them. One even snapped pictures with an old-school camera.

Clint and I followed the horse back towards the apartment building, toward the man with the root beer.

"Here, take this." The neighbor handed Clint the extension cord and extended the soda out to the horse.

The horse bared his teeth and bit at the edge of the can gingerly. Once it had the lip of the soda firmly between its teeth, it wrapped its lips against the can and flung its head upwards.

Then it started sucking. The soda sieved between its teeth, causing a gush of root beer froth.

My mouth dropped open. Clint grimaced. A few of the reporters broke out in laughter.

The horse swallowed in big gulps, the foam billowing at the sides of its mouth and sluicing past its enormous jowls, then down its neck.

Clint fashioned the cord into a loose ring—not quite a lasso, not quite a collar—and looped it around the horse's neck, then handed the other end to the neighbor.

One hand on the cord, the other scratching himself, the neighbor said, "I'll hang onto him until the kids get home."

"Who's the Horse Whisperer now?" I asked Clint, shaking my head as we walked toward the entry.

"Learn something new every day," he replied, grinning.

AFTER CLIMBING the stairwell to the third floor, we knocked on Nancy's door.

"Hi, Nancy?" Clint said gently when it was opened by a woman around my age. "I'm Detective McKenna, and this is Macy Ellis. She's a nurse consultant, working with our department. We called earlier."

"Yes. Of course," she whispered. "Please come in."

Nancy's eyes were red and puffy, but she managed a weak smile as she led us into her apartment, a chaotic reflection of a life that had been turned upside down in the last day and a half.

The small living room was cluttered with mismatched furniture, including a threadbare armchair that seemed to have lost a fight with a cat, and a rickety bookshelf overflowing with self-help books, romance novels, and a collection of porcelain cat figurines. A faded pink carpet with wrinkles at the doorways covered the floor. The walls were a shrine to Cara, plastered with her childhood drawings and school awards, as well as candid snapshots that captured the fleeting moments of happiness before tragedy struck. The air was thick with the scent of stale cigarette smoke and the lingering aroma of reheated leftovers.

As we began talking, I learned that my mother was right, we had attended the same high school in the late nineties, although we didn't know each other back then.

"Do you remember the Christmas dance in '97?" Nancy asked, forcing a sad chuckle. "The DJ's equipment malfunctioned, and all we could dance to was the *Titanic* theme song on repeat."

I nodded, my own laughter tinged with sadness. "I remember that. It was awful, but we all tried to make the best of it as it evolved into an impromptu ballet performance. I still have trouble getting that song out of my head sometimes."

Beneath the surface of our shared memories, the unspoken tragedy of her daughter hung heavy in the air. "I'm so sorry for your loss, Nancy," I said finally, my voice a whisper. "We'll do everything we can to find out what happened to Cara."

"Is Cara's father here?" Clint asked.

"He's not a part of our life." Nancy spoke quickly and her body language tightened like the subject was unpleasant. "Before you ask, no, he's not involved. Has never been in her life. He's a pro baseball player in South Korea. Had a game on TV the night when..." she trailed off.

Clint took notes. Probably a detail he'd want to double check.

I thought of Bruce having left me while I was pregnant with Bridget. Would we have been lonely if Kenny hadn't joined our little family unit? We'd have had more money, *definitely*. But would we have had as much laughter and joy?

"Are you here alone?" I asked her. "Can we call someone to come be with you?"

Nancy nodded, tears welling up in her eyes again. "Thank you. My sister is here, she's sleeping in my room right now, she was up with me all night. We're okay. We're okay."

Clint glanced at his watch, clearly wanting to be sensitive but also wanting to get into the reason we were here. "Can I ask you some questions about Cara?"

Nancy didn't say anything, but she nodded, almost imperceptibly.

As I listened, Clint asked Nancy a series of questions, starting with general things about Cara and her life.

Nineteen years old, Cara had been raised with a lot of love but little money, and her life was about to take off. She'd gotten past the first round of interviews at Unity Airways and enrolled in flight attendant school. Her ticket to fly to Houston for her training would never be used. When she'd been killed, she was three days from her last shift at the consignment shop she'd worked at for three years.

Her Instagram bio was one sentence long: *Adventurer, looking forward to exploring the greater world once I get my wings.*

"Was she dating anyone?" Clint asked after a long pause.

"No. Not that I know of."

"And what about close friends, favorite teachers or mentors?"

As Nancy searched her memory for the names of friends Cara had mentioned, I listened for a crucial piece of information that would unlock the mystery of her death, some little clue or long-lost name that would break the case wide open. Clearly, I'd watched too many TV shows, because what I got instead were the meandering recollections of a devastated mom who'd been doing her best as a single parent and was now doing her best just to stay upright.

When the conversation hit a pause as Clint wrote notes in

his notebook, I leaned forward, hands clasped in my lap. "Nancy, is there anything else you can tell us? Anything at all that might help us understand what happened to Cara?"

Nancy hesitated, her eyes darting away for a moment. When she looked back at us, she continued, "Well, there is one thing," she began, her voice trembling. "But I don't know if it's important or not."

I exchanged glances with Clint. "Please, Nancy," I urged. "Anything could help."

"Well..." she picked up a pack of cigarettes, frowned when she discovered it was empty, then set it gently back on the table. "She was never supposed to be in the park that night."

CHAPTER 11

"Good," Clint said, "Let's start there. Can you walk us through the day, the evening?"

As Nancy wiped away tears, she began to recount the details of her daughter's last night. "Cara was out with her friends at the beach in Hansville, just enjoying the evening." Her voice trembled with both anger and sorrow. "They got ice cream at that Hansville Cafe place. I don't know what it's called, but it's the only real restaurant there."

"The Hansville Café, General Store, and Bait Shop," I said. "When the new guy bought it a couple years ago, they had to buy a new sign to fit the whole name."

Nancy chuckled sadly, then pulled out her phone to show us a photo. "She texted me this picture. She was posing with the cutest corgi." The image showed Cara crouched down, the beach in the background, an ice cream cone in one hand as she smiled brightly alongside the happy little dog. The dog's tongue stuck out the side of its mouth and looked as though, when stretched, it would be as long as nearly half the length of its extra long body.

"What time was the photo sent?" Clint asked.

Nancy looked at the message. "7:42 PM. She dropped off her friends at their house after that, and she was supposed to be home by eight to watch *Abbott Elementary*. Cara wasn't into partying or drinking, you know? She was more of a... a nerd, I guess. She was studying to be a veterinarian, planned to become a flight attendant to pay her way through veterinary school."

As Nancy spoke, the room seemed to close in on us, the weight of her grief suffocating.

"I never heard from her again. The officer who… who told me… said she was killed around 8:30 PM that night."

Nancy's voice broke and she buried her head in her hands.

I did the math in my head. If Cara had sent the photo at 7:42 PM, then taken her friends home in Hansville, she hadn't had time to do much else before stopping at the lake.

Clint spoke up, his voice gentle but firm. "We've already interviewed Cara's friends and the store owner, and they confirmed everything you said. The GPS on Cara's car corroborated the story, too. Arrived at the lake at 8:14 PM. We don't know why she took a detour to Buck Lake Park instead of coming straight home."

A silence fell over the room as we all sat with the unasked question. My heart ached for Nancy, and I could see Clint's jaw tighten, a sign of his own frustration. Each time I blinked, I saw the picture in my mind's eye: Cara posing with an ice cream cone and a cute little corgi, happy as a clam only forty-five minutes before being strangled a mile away from where the photo was taken. Just like happens with nursing, this job was going to chew up my heart.

Fortunately, my years as a nurse had rendered my heart the texture of undercooked chuck roast. I was pretty tough.

Ninety percent of me wanted to get up and get out of there, to avoid the grief that seemed to be spilling out of Nancy into me. Thankfully, the other ten percent of me kept my butt on the sofa, able to ask the next question. "What could have made her go to the park? Was it somewhere you'd been before?" After a pause, I put it another way. "I guess the key thing is, did she just drop by on her own, or did someone lure her there?"

Nancy shook her head, her eyes welling up with tears again. "I don't know. Cara wasn't the type to just wander off. She wasn't especially spontaneous. She was responsible and always kept her word. I mean, maybe she stopped to take a selfie or something, but..."

I nodded, sharing in her confusion. My mind raced with possibilities, trying to find some clue or connection that would lead us to the truth.

"Store owner said he hadn't seen anyone suspicious," Clint said. "And he remembered Cara's friends. Guy is retired NYPD, so his observations were sharp. We don't believe she was followed from the store."

"She *loved* taking selfies," Nancy said, voice wavering as she speculated about Cara's visit to the lake. "Especially during sunset and next to water. It was kind of her... I don't know, her guilty pleasure, I guess. She'd pose and post them on Instagram. Officer said they didn't find her phone, and the last thing she posted on Instagram was the same photo with the dog. The one I showed you."

Clint fell quiet and I heard myself asking, "Do you have any connection to Jared Norris or... have you heard of him?" I regretted the question right away.

Nancy furrowed her brow, searching her memory as she again picked up the empty cigarette pack. "No, I don't think so. I mean, wait, is that the Waxlace Strangler case? I remember hearing about it, but it was a long time ago." She paused, eyes narrowing, and suddenly crumpled the pack in her hand. "Wait. Why are you asking me that? He's in prison for the rest of his life, isn't he?"

The heavy silence Clint and I responded with was enough to answer her question.

"What do you *know*?" she shouted. "Why aren't you telling me? You can't, can you?" The room crackled with tension as Nancy's grief transformed into anger. "You can't tell me because you let out a murderer. Oh God, *you've* murdered my daughter."

Clint raised his hands in a calming gesture. "Nancy, we're looking at all angles of the case, I promise you. Jared Norris is being pursued as a suspect. We don't yet know who is to blame for the death of your daughter."

"*Murder*, of my daughter," she corrected. Nancy seemed to wrestle with her emotions for a moment before responding between clenched teeth with a more tempered voice. "I just want to know the truth. I want to know who did this to my daughter, and I want them to pay."

"We can't possibly understand what you are going through," I said, my voice soft but steady. "We're doing everything we can to find answers. I shouldn't have brought that up because... we really don't know. That was out of line, and I'm sorry."

Nancy didn't say anything.

The interview was teetering on the edge of a cliff, but before anyone could say anything else, Clint's phone buzzed. He glanced at the screen, his expression serious. He cocked his head while reading it, then handed me the phone.

It was a text from a contact called *Mike, Seattle PD,* and read, "Jared Norris is at the main branch of the Seattle Public library. We'll keep an eye on him until you get there."

I handed Clint his phone, then reached out and touched Nancy gently on the hand. "We're going to go interview Jared now. Nancy... Nancy are you hearing me?"

She looked up slowly. "Just please... find him, find who did this."

I squeezed her hand. "I promise you this, Nancy, I'll pursue this like I would if it was my own daughter."

PART II
COGNITIVE DISSONANCE

CHAPTER 12

IT WAS late afternoon by the time we pulled up to the main branch of the Seattle Public Library. Rain splattered against the windshield and created a watercolor effect on the building's impressive glass facade. Clint parked the car and we sat for a moment, gathering our thoughts before heading inside. His phone rang, the shrill sound slicing the silence.

Clint picked it up and put it on speaker.

"Hey, guys," Carlo said, his voice tinged with exhaustion. "We've got a couple things to report."

I leaned in closer, eager to hear what they had found.

Maria chimed in, her voice more energetic than Carlo's. "First, the evidence team at Area One found a size ten men's shoeprint about a hundred yards from where the body was found. It's not much, but it's something. They'll be searching the area for at least another day. The killer seems to have covered most of his tracks, but he might've slipped up with this one."

Clint nodded. "Thanks, Maria. Keep us updated if you find anything else."

"Actually, there *is* something else," she said. "We got the results from the wax analysis. Turns out it's a bee's wax. Same kind they use for winter sports shoe laces. Same kind that was found on the necks of the three girls murdered in Seattle twenty years ago. We have to get to the records from the original case to see if they are exact matches, but it's definitely the same MO."

A shiver ran down my spine, my heart rate accelerating. The connection was undeniable. The Waxlace Strangler was back, or someone was copying him. I felt my fists clenching and had to force myself to relax.

When Clint ended the call, he glanced over at me. "Ready?"

I nodded and followed him out of the car, hurrying through the warm August rain into the inviting library. Making my way through the stacks of books and rows of computers, the familiar smell of old paper and ink filled my nostrils, and for a moment, the weight of the case seemed a little lighter.

We walked towards a private research room, where we'd been informed Jared would be.

As we entered, I spotted him huddled over a book on rare birds of the Pacific Northwest. He looked even more gaunt and creepy than I remembered, dressed entirely in white—white jeans, white t-shirt, and a pair of white sneakers. It was eerie, like he was a specter haunting the library.

As we approached, he looked up, his eyes locking onto mine. A flicker of recognition crossed his face, and he immediately smiled and addressed me. "Macy Ellis, right? I remember you. You wrote articles about me."

I nodded slowly. I was surprised he recognized me.

"That's right, Jared," Clint said. "We're here to ask you some questions."

During his trial, Jared had been diagnosed with both severe obsessive compulsive disorder and schizophrenia. Many people —including prosecutors, the families of the victims, and members of the press—thought he was faking it. I didn't know either way, but the jury agreed with the defense and sent him to psychiatric prison. Now, his outfit and odd mannerisms made me suspicious. If he wasn't a crazed murderer *before* he went to psychiatric prison, he damn sure might be one now. His white on white on white outfit made for a backdrop that highlighted his every gesture. His fingers moved one at a time, like a hand model protecting freshly painted fingernails before a photo-shoot. He crossed his legs and tapped his feet incessantly, like a kid who needed to use the bathroom.

Clint leaned in, his voice low and menacing. "What's your shoe size, Jared?"

Jared looked puzzled. "Size ten. Why does that matter?"

"The same size shoeprint was found at a crime scene across the Sound in Area One," Clint replied, scrutinizing Jared's face for any hint of guilt. "You been to Buck Lake Park recently?"

"What crime scene?" Jared asked. He looked toward me, but his eyes were focused three inches above and ten feet behind my head.

Clint just glared at him, as though he might break him with the simple force of his psychic will.

"Jared," I said, "we already know that police questioned you regarding the murder of the teenaged girl across the water." I decided to take a softer approach, hoping to gain his trust. "I remember writing about your case years ago. I know you've been through a lot, but we just want to find the truth."

His eyes flicked toward mine, then he resumed his distant stare. "You were my only hope, Macy." For a moment, his paranoia seemed to dissipate. "You still are. Thank you for believing me."

I hesitated, taken aback by his gratitude. In reality, I *hadn't* supported him; I'd merely written an article citing sources within the police department who questioned his guilt at the time of his arrest. Now, seeing the man before me, I wondered if questioning his guilt had been wrong.

Clint pressed on, relentless. "So, Jared, where were you on Tuesday, the night the girl was killed?"

"At the library, until closing time," he answered, his voice shaking. "I left at 8 pm."

"It takes a minimum of an hour and fifteen minutes to get from here to Hansville," I said. "And that's with perfect ferry timing and some exceeding the speed limit." I glanced at Clint. "We know that Cara was killed around 8:30 pm."

Jared's eyes widened. "You still think I did it, don't you?" His paranoia returned in full force. "That's why you're here!" Jared's muscles tensed away from us, like a cat poised to spring towards its prey.

Clint raised a hand, trying to calm him. "We're just trying to verify your alibi, Jared. We'll be checking the library's security footage to make sure everything lines up."

"And if it does," I interjected, trying to gauge his reaction, "if it does, then we know it's not possible for you to be the killer."

Jared's face contorted, a mix of fear and anger. "You'll see me on that footage, Bird as my witness. You won't find anything because I didn't do it! I was locked up for twenty years, accused of crimes I never committed." His breathing grew faster and faster as he spoke. "And now, you're trying to pin this on me too?"

I exchanged a glance with Clint, uncertain how to proceed.

Clint let out a sigh that made me think he believed Jared was a good actor. "Let's check out the footage," he said.

"Jared," I said softly, "we're just doing our job. We need to follow every lead and rule out every possibility. If you're innocent, the truth will come out."

He stared at me, his eyes wild and desperate. "The truth? I've been waiting for the truth for two decades, and it hasn't done me any good. What makes you think it'll be different this time?"

I had no answer for him.

CHAPTER 13

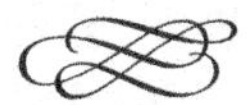

THE SEATTLE PUBLIC LIBRARY was a bustling sanctuary of knowledge. As Clint and I walked through the aisles, the Dewey Decimal System labels brought back memories of afternoons spent at my local library as a teenager, seeking solace in literature. Something about those small, orderly stickers on the spines of books made me yearn for a simpler time. Before parenthood, debt, cellphones and, most of all, before Kenny.

Jared, attempting to be stealthy, followed us through the stacks. His movements were far from subtle, and I could sense his eyes on us as we navigated the library. His lurking presence was unnerving, to say the least.

We approached the front desk and spoke with a friendly librarian who led us to Laney, the head of library security. She was a short, muscular woman with a uniform that looked a tad too tight, making her appear even more compact.

Laney's office was dusty and spare, an odd contrast to the vast collection of books just outside her door. Her desk was dominated by a computer displaying four windows of video monitoring. Two of the screens showed bookshelves, one captured activity outside the bathroom doors, and the fourth revealed the front of the library.

Questioned by Clint, she explained that she could easily show us anything that had occurred within the last month. As we listened to her, I noticed the tension in Clint's posture, betraying his eagerness to examine the footage.

Just then, I saw Jared peering through the window of the office. Laney noticed him, too, and said, "That guy is always here."

Clint and I exchanged glances, silently acknowledging the strangeness of his constant presence. I decided to break the silence. "Laney, we'd like to review the footage from the night Cara Thompson was killed. The night before last. Can you help us with that?"

"Of course," Laney replied, her fingers flying over the keyboard as she pulled up the relevant footage. "What exactly are you looking for?"

Clint gestured towards Jared. "We want to know what time this guy left the library on Tuesday night. He says he left at closing time, 8 PM. We want to confirm."

"Like I told the other officers, he's here until eight most days. I mean, ever since he was released. Ask me, guys like him should be executed." She sighed. "But I don't get to make that call, do I? The state says he served his time and, as a card carrying member of the King County Library System, he's entitled to be here."

As the video played, Clint and I watched intently. Laney fast-forwarded through a few hours of footage, pausing every once in a while to confirm Jared's presence.

Jared flipping through a book.

Jared entering the bathroom.

Jared returning to the book.

"Three o'clock 'til just before seven, when he went up to the research stacks," Laney said. "Top floor."

"No footage of him leaving?" I asked.

"No," she replied, "And none of him after seven, it seems."

"He couldn't have just disappeared." I couldn't help but state the obvious.

Laney rolled her eyes. "See, we only keep video on our rare and valuable sections. And of course, the new releases. Oh, and also the religious section, sometimes people steal books to suppress a viewpoint. There's a camera there too. But he could have walked down the stairwell from the research stacks and gone out the back door."

Clint leaned in, his eyes searching Laney's face. "We're hoping to speak with the employee who reported that Jared was at the library through closing on the night in question. Can you help us with that?"

A troubled expression crossed Laney's face. "Well, the thing is, the kid didn't show up for his last shift. It's not the first time, though. He's disappeared before." She paused, hesitating before continuing. "His coworkers suspect that he and his mother are homeless. They think he vanishes sometimes to take care of her or when he can't find transportation."

Clint and I exchanged glances, our concern for the young employee mingling with our frustration at the investigation's latest hurdle.

We took a copy of the video and thanked Laney for her assistance, then stepped out of her office, back into the maze of bookshelves. Clint's brow was furrowed. "Anything on the video look shady to you?"

I shook my head. "Nah, but you'd know better than I would."

"I don't think so. I mean, he could've hacked into the system, used AI or something, but..." he trailed off.

"Yeah, doesn't seem like the type," I said.

As we made our way toward the exit, we passed Jared again. He was sitting by himself at one of the tables in the non-fiction stacks. He stared at me with a face that I could only describe as disturbed. I was chilled to the bone and hurried my steps to stay as close to Clint as possible, nearly tripping us both.

Outside the library, it had stopped raining. As we left, we were greeted by the unexpected sight and sound of a string instrument. Played by a woman sitting on the sidewalk just outside the entrance, the instrument had a long wooden neck adorned with two strings, stretching down to a small resonator at the base that she rested on her thigh. It made sweeping notes similar to a violin as she pulled a bow over the strings. The mesmerizing melody it produced stopped us in our tracks, a hauntingly beautiful sound that heightened the uneasy feeling Jared had left me with.

I glanced at Clint and he seemed as captivated as I was. He reached into his wallet, pulling out a five-dollar bill and placing it in the purse that sat open at her feet.

She looked up, her eyes filled with gratitude. She mouthed the words "Thank you," her fingers and bow never ceasing their dance across the instrument.

As we continued to our car, the sound of the music still lingering in the air, I felt a growing sense of unease. The investigation was getting more complicated. Twenty years ago, I thought Jared might be innocent, but he'd had no alibi and had been convicted.

Now he seemed guilty as sin but had what could end up being an airtight alibi. If the library employee confirmed that he'd been in the research stacks until eight, there was no way he was our killer.

As we pulled away from the library, I looked back at the woman playing her instrument, the haunting melody echoing in my mind, a reminder of the questions still waiting to be answered.

“I need to eat,” Clint said. “Do you need to eat?”

A pang of hunger hit me. I remembered the peanut-buttered english muffin I'd made myself for breakfast that morning. I didn't recall finishing it and I couldn't remember if I had left the remainder of it sitting at the auto repair shop or on the kitchen counter at home. Somehow I hadn't remembered to eat lunch either. I may not have had a valid nursing license, but I still ate like a nurse halfway through a double shift at the emergency room—stuffing any random food into my face on a three minute break before rushing back to help my patients and their families through what could be the worst day of their life.

I returned from my mind drift and faintly remembered I had been asked a question. "I absolutely *do* need to eat."

CHAPTER 14

IT WAS past ten when Clint pulled to a stop on Alaskan Way in downtown Seattle. "Ferry leaves in half an hour," he said, idling the car at the back of the taxi stand. "Want me to wait with you for a few?"

I nodded. Looking west, past the parking lot, the dark waters of the Puget Sound seemed vast and ominous, somehow intimidating me despite the fact that I'd taken the short ferry ride thousands of times before. Maybe it was just that I didn't feel like being alone.

We'd spent the last two hours at a fancy Italian restaurant Clint had "been meaning to try." When I say there's an Italian place I've been "meaning to try," that might mean that a friend had told me they had good meatballs. To Clint, it meant the new Michelin star restaurant guide had come out, and he had $500 he wanted to blow on dinner for two. It also meant a six-course tasting menu that included dishes like *tortellini en brodo with white Alba truffle*, and *sea bass tartare with capers and Meyer lemon vinaigrette*. By the time we were through, I knew more about regional Italian cuisine than a well-traveled recipe box. Clint had offered to pay, his *welcome-to-the-job* treat, but the way he savored the food—the way he *talked about* the food—made me think he'd missed his calling as a restaurant critic.

The silence in the car was beginning to feel awkward. "Where are you staying tonight?" I asked. At dinner he'd told me he planned to stay over in Seattle for an early morning meeting with a buddy from the SPD.

"The Royal Mayflower," he said. "I'll be starting my day with freshly brewed artisanal coffee and Japanese-style soufflé pancakes." He smacked his lips. "Only thing better than a gourmet dinner is a gourmet dinner followed by a gourmet breakfast the next morning."

"You're an odd man, Clint." The whole meal, I'd had to bite my tongue to avoid breaking his rule: *don't ask about my past or my family*. At some point, I had to find out how a guy like him had ended up as a WSP detective.

"Thank you." After letting that sit for a moment, he asked, "You got a taxi home on the other side?"

I nodded. "Ordered it between the third and fourth courses. Also talked to my mom. She's letting Gonzo have his first sleep-over. Told me he's already gained *second grandchild* status in her heart."

"Sometimes I look around at the world and think, *we don't deserve dogs*."

I cocked my head. "Would have thought you'd think we don't deserve horses."

"Oh, we *definitely* don't deserve horses." He smiled. "So your mom'll bring you to the office tomorrow?"

"Yeah. She has some errands to run. So, it works." We'd skipped the wine pairing with dinner, so we weren't tipsy, but my head was spinning. Along with the ominous feeling the dark waters were throwing at me, it felt strange to be sitting alone in a car with him, light rain pattering the roof. It had been the strangest two days of my life and now, here I was, sitting in a car next to a good-looking man who'd just bought me a very *expensive* dinner.

He was a hard guy to read. Or maybe I'd just lost all my abilities in that department.

Clint looked around the car, then glanced in my direction. His eyes scanned from my face to my chest, then down to my feet. Was he looking me up and down?

Even though part of my brain knew he wasn't about to kiss me, another part wondered if he was. After being single for a year and having married Bruce so young, and Kenny so soon after that, my flirtation gauge needed service.

"Have you seen my phone?" His voice snapped me out of it.

It was vibrating.

It had fallen on the floor.

I cleared my throat, embarrassed. Fumbling, I handed it to him.

He answered, keeping the call private by not putting it on speakerphone. I tried not to eavesdrop, but curiosity and concern got the better of me.

"Yeah," Clint muttered, his face growing increasingly serious. "Hmm."

I glanced at him, my stomach knotting with anxiety as I listened to his side of the conversation.

"That's not good," he said, his voice tight. I watched his fingers grip the steering wheel, knuckles blanching.

The call seemed to stretch on forever. Cars began to drive onto the ferry, which was my cue that it was time to hop out and walk on.

Finally, Clint hung up and turned to me, his expression grave.

"Jared has a ten o'clock curfew as part of his parole," he explained, his voice tense. "He didn't check in electronically from his home, and they don't know where he is."

I glanced at the digital clock on his dashboard. It was 10:35 PM.

I swallowed hard, my heart pounding in my chest. "Do you think we spooked him?" I asked. "Maybe he fled. Or do you think he could be…" I glanced out the back windshield. "He wouldn't be coming after us? Would he?"

"You'll be safe, Macy. You're not the killer's victim type. And, with the all white Jared was wearing today, you'd see him coming a mile away." Clint could see I had fear written all over my face. "Besides. Strange as he was, I don't think he's our guy on this."

"Yeah, but even so, if *he* thinks that *we* think he is…" I stopped myself, taking a breath. "I'm sure they'll find him soon," I managed to say.

I opened the door and got out, then leaned my head back in through the open door. "I'll see you tomorrow, Clint. Thanks for an interesting day and a fantastic dinner."

Climbing the stairs to the main passenger cabin, I could feel the sense of nostalgia wash over me. The Washington State ferry had a certain charm to it—the faint scent of diesel mixed with the salty sea air, the rhythmic hum of the engine, and the sturdy, no-nonsense design.

The well-worn seats, mostly empty at this hour, had seen countless passengers and heard countless stories. The nighttime view of the Seattle skyline was breathtaking, with the Space Needle standing tall against a backdrop of twinkling stars, and the inky black water reflecting the dazzling city lights.

Wandering the mostly empty cabin, I was reminded of a time when I had ridden this very ferry with my father. He was on a rare adventure outside of his workshop doing me a favor, moving a large curio cabinet that my paternal grandmother had bequeathed to me.

He *might* have done it without the fried chicken dinner I promised to make him. After all, he did like being the hero. But it was our ritual for me to ask him for help paid for with a culinary bribe.

It was a beautiful piece, with intricate carvings and glass doors, but it had also become a symbol of the difficult decision I was grappling with at the time. Both the cabinet and myself were fragile objects that might shatter into a billion pieces with the next rogue wave.

I had been working as a journalist in the city, but was leaving it all behind to attend nursing school and support my husband's dream of opening an auto repair shop. Homeward bound riding the Wenatchee that day, wind whipping through my hair on the top deck of the ferry, the weight of my decision hung heavy on my shoulders. The weight of Bridget—who was still in utero—hung heavy at my front. Tears welled up in my eyes as I struggled to hold them back. My father, never one for emotional conversations, sensed my distress and did what he always did when things got tough: he told a lame dad joke.

"Why does a ferry boat never get sick?" he asked, a playful glint in his eye.

I sniffled, wiping away a stray tear. "I don't know, Dad. Why?"

"Because it's always going to the dock!" He laughed, his shoulders shaking with mirth.

As much as I rolled my eyes at his terrible jokes, they always managed to make me laugh until my cheeks hurt. At that moment, surrounded by the vast expanse of water and the comforting presence of my father, I felt just a little bit lighter. And I embraced my decision with more hope.

Snapping back to the present, I grabbed a bag of chips from the vending machine—because who *doesn't* need a bag of paper-thin chips after a six-course tasting menu?—and chose a seat by the window. But before I sat, something stopped me. A feeling, maybe a glint of light in the huge picture windows. A prickling sensation crawled up my spine. I couldn't shake the feeling that the man behind me was watching me. I placed a chip on my tongue and let the fatty saltiness dissolve until biting into it made no crunch. Then did the same with another.

My nerves were already frayed from the news about Jared, and I couldn't tell if my paranoia was justified, or just a product of my overactive imagination. I knew it wasn't Jared—the reflection I'd seen briefly had been shorter, stockier, but I didn't want to fully look in his direction to take in the details. Regardless, I decided to do a lap around the seating area, trying to appear casual as I scanned the faces of the few passengers who were still awake, nursing my bag of chips as I walked.

I wandered past the vending machines and out the cabin doors on the main passenger level, taking in the breathtaking view of the water from the observation area. Even behind the outdoor windows meant to shield passengers from the bulk of the wind, the cold current of air whipped my hair into my face, making my eyes water. I blinked away the tears, straining to see. The man had come to the deck as well, remaining at a distance just far enough to keep me wondering whether I was being stalked.

The moonlight cast eerie shadows across the deck, heightening my unease.

Retracing my steps back into the cabin's main seating area, my heart pounded in my chest. Was I truly being watched, or was it just the stress of the day playing tricks on me?

I hesitated for a moment before climbing the staircase to the top deck, my heart pounding as I listened for footsteps I couldn't possibly hear above the roar of the engines. Too scared to turn around, I quickened my pace, the cold wind biting at my cheeks and turning the tips of my ears numb.

Reaching the top deck, I hurried over to a small group of people huddled together against the railing, seeking comfort in their presence. The footsteps I couldn't hear seemed to be closing in, and my breath caught in my throat.

I couldn't keep running from my fears. Gathering my courage, I turned to face the man who, by now, I was certain was following me.

To my relief, it wasn't Jared. I mean, I'd known it wasn't Jared, but somehow still thought it might be. But that didn't make the stranger's appearance any less unsettling.

He wore what looked like an expensive business suit, face and hands revealing light brown skin that looked like it had been artificially tanned. He had wild, dyed-blond hair that danced in the cool wind. One thing I was sure of was that I'd never seen him before.

Our eyes locked for a brief, intense moment, and then he turned and walked away without a word.

My heart still racing, I leaned against the railing, cursing my own carelessness. I felt vulnerable and exposed, the darkness of the night pressing in on me from all sides. The only thing I could do was stay close to the crowd and try to self soothe by finishing the bag of chips. Why hadn't I found a way to deal with my cell phone bill? Not that I would have any cell service way out in the middle of the Puget Sound, but still.

It was just some dude, I told myself. Maybe he was trying to approach me to get my number. After all, I wasn't wearing a coffee-stained robe, and I'd managed not to spill any Italian food on my shirt. I chuckled. Maybe once he got a closer look and saw me nervously clutching my potato chip bag, he'd thought twice about getting to know me.

I finished the last chip, feeling bummed out and exhausted. They never have the right amount of chips in a bag. A small bag is too small and the large bags are too big. I wanted my goldilocks portion. There isn't a word for it in English, but on a trip to the Japanese gardens in Portland I'd learned the word *kuchisabishii.* The small chip bags are not big enough to satisfy a lonely mouth. It wasn't that I was hungry, it was just that I wanted something to distract me from my feelings.

I folded the bag so that no chip remnants or grease could spill from it and jammed it into my pocket.

As I scanned my surroundings, my senses remained on high alert. I tried to convince myself that I was overreacting, that my fear was the product of an overactive imagination fueled by the day's events. But as I stood there, my back pressed against the cold metal railing and the wind howling around me, I couldn't shake the feeling that something was very wrong. And as the ferry continued its steady journey across the dark waters, I knew that I had to remain vigilant, but not paranoid. It was a fine line.

Taking a deep breath, I forced myself to focus on the beauty of the night. The city lights shimmered on the water's surface, creating a mesmerizing, almost otherworldly, scene. The stars above seemed brighter and more numerous than I'd ever noticed before, and I tried to lose myself in their brilliance, if only for a moment. There was something magical about being out on the water, surrounded by the vast expanse of the Puget Sound. It was a place where the line between the ordinary and the extraordinary seemed to blur.

And it was there, amidst the darkness and wild beauty of the night, that I felt a renewed sense of determination to help Clint and the team find Cara's killer.

CHAPTER 15

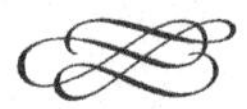

I AWOKE THE NEXT MORNING, brain buzzing with an idea.

As I stumbled into the kitchen for coffee, rubbing sleep from my eyes, I remembered the small storage unit my husband and I had rented in Kingston, just a short drive from my house.

I had protested the rental, but couldn't refuse when Kenny brought home a dozen car seats he'd obtained at an auction in Clallam County and plopped them down on our living room floor, couch, and coffee table. It seemed he had one seat for every make and model of car.

"These will be great," he'd said. "I got them for a steal. Next time someone drives in an Audi with white leather interior, or a Ford Explorer with dark gray cloth interior, we match them with one of these seats and *blammo,* cashola!"

Of course, the seats had ended up being just as profitable as his investment in the Greater Kitsap Pigeon Racing League. Which is to say, I had to work weekends for a month to pay for them. They'd ended up jammed into the storage unit collecting dust with a few boxes of old paperwork and other keepsakes. Like a lot of things from my time with Kenny, I'd tried to block those car seats, and the storage unit, from my mind.

But now I thought it might be the home of the remaining documents from my past as a journalist in Seattle. Only problem was, I was sure that by now I would be locked out of the storage unit for non-payment. One of the envelopes on my desk was probably a notice to vacate.

There was a knock at the door. “Mac, it’s me.”

My mother. Half an hour earlier than we’d agreed.

Dorothy had her own sense of time. When I was a teenager she would often drop me off early and pick me up late. *Unless* she had taken me somewhere she didn’t especially want me to be. Then she would tend to drop me off late and pick me up early.

Now her routine was to show up early and never leave.

I could see where she was coming from. We do whatever we can to get to spend time with our grown daughters. If we don’t break down their doors trying to be with them, we might not get to opine over their every life decision.

With a sigh, I let her in and put on some coffee. Gonzo was folded under her arm and she took her usual spot, on the living room side of the kitchen in the open floorplan of my house. Walls only served to block the view on a beachfront house like mine. The fewer the walls, the grander the view of the Salish Sea.

“What is this?” I asked.

Something was different about Gonzo’s bed.

“I did some alterations. See?”

My mother had sewn straps to either side of the dog bed, using wide pink satin ribbons so it could be carried like a purse. She had also sewn up the small hole where the stuffing had been threatening to escape.

“I couldn’t let us risk dropping our little angel, could I?” As she said this, she patted Gonzo on the head and cooed at him. The tiny dog blinked his eyes rapidly and lifted his head to be scritched under the chin while obsessively lapping at my mother's fingers like they were fountains of secret sauce.

I had difficulty imagining my neighbor Bob giving Gonzo this kind of gentle affection, but the dog appeared appreciative and not unused to the attention.

"The purse is clever, Ma," I had to agree.

Her phone rang and she rolled her eyes. "It's your dad." Then, accepting the call, she said, "I'm with Macy, and you're on speaker. What's up?"

"You're at Macy's? She seen my quarter-inch socket extension?"

She rolled her eyes even harder this time.

"No, dad," I said. "Why on God's green earth would I have seen your quarter-inch socket extension?"

My father's tools functioned as an extension of his body, and I could almost feel his disappointment through the phone.

"Hmm... thought maybe Kenny took it," he grumbled. "Mac, you get a date yet?"

"No, no date," I called, grabbing the eggs from the fridge.

"Well make sure you snag someone who won't borrow my tools. Next time marry a writer or something, will ya?"

This time I was sure I could hear my mother's eyes rolling. "Go find some dirt and dig it," my mother scolded, ending the call.

"Wait, why did he call in the first place?" I asked.

My mom smiled. "Probably to ask what I left him for lunch and to see if he can rip out my hydrangeas to dig another hole in the yard. He can find his own food. And he's gonna find me putting a hole in *him* if moves my hydrangeas."

When he wasn't up in his shop looking for his unreturned tools, my father liked to dig holes all over the property. Of course, he always had a good reason for a particular hole: Gotta put a pond over here. Working on the septic over there. Your mother wants a submerged greenhouse back there. The greenhouse he'd dug for her was his hole in the ground pièce de résistance. He'd dug a pond in the center. *That* had required digging a hole in the dirt *with a dirt hole* dug into it.

I pulled out a frying pan and began to cook some scrambled eggs. "Rye or white?" I asked.

"Are you asking me or Gonzo?"

"Mom, I'm sure that Gonzo will eat whatever kind of bread I offer him as long as it's offered while he is sitting near my plate at the dining table."

"I don't know, he got picky with me last night."

"What were you trying to feed him?" I asked.

"We had chicken and sweet potatoes."

"Sounds like something he would like," I said.

"He liked it but the minute he had a bite of those sweet potatoes he didn't want to touch any more chicken. Little guy took a piece of chicken I offered, walked across the table and spat it over the table and onto the floor. He did that twice! Gave him a bite of sweet potato and…" she turned back to Gonzo and put on her sweet, babying voice… "You ate that greedily, *didn't you my little sweet potato*." Looking up, she said, "He might be a stubborn little spud, but now he is *our* stubborn little spud."

I rolled my eyes. "I'm making us rye."

As I put the bread in the toaster, I thought about what I might find in the storage unit. Notebooks, photos, and mementos stacked on the car seats. Maybe I would find something useful for the case. My hope was that I hadn't waited too long and the owners hadn't destroyed or auctioned off the contents.

My mother, Gonzo, and I ate our breakfast at high speed, then headed out for a quick stop at The Wrench King. I was pleasantly surprised to find that, for once, things were running smoothly. No angry customers or unexpected crises, just the familiar hum of machinery and the smell of grease, rubber, and welded metal fumes.

I stepped into my cluttered office and grabbed the stack of mail, then returned to my mother's car. Hoping I wouldn't find a notice from the storage unit company, I thumbed through the stack.

"Mac, oh my, Mac." My mom repeatedly shifted her eyes from the road to scrutinize my neglected mail pile. "How long has it been since you opened your mail?"

"Ma, I can't have the 'I'm disappointed in you' talk right now." I continued to flip through the envelopes, gathering the ones I would keep between my fingers in the order of their importance and collecting the ones I would later trash into the passenger side door pocket. "Please," I continued absentmindedly. "Can you just let me fail at life in peace?"

As she drove, grudgingly holding her tongue, I continued through the stack. Most of it was bills that could wait, or *would* wait even if they couldn't. And junk mail. Nothing from the storage unit yet, which gave me some hope.

One envelope caught my eye, a letter from Florida.

Curiosity piqued, I tucked the 'keepers' between my knees and opened the Florida envelope. "Kenny, you beautiful bastard," I said.

"What?" my mom asked.

Inside the envelope were five crisp hundred-dollar bills and a short, handwritten note. It read: *Least I can do. I'm sorry.*

"What?" she repeated. "Your nursing license or..." She glanced down and saw the money. "Oh."

"He sent a little money. That's all." I was careful to shield the note from my mother, I didn't want any more questions than I was already getting.

My first instinct was anger, a familiar heat rising in my chest at the thought of where his flaws had left me. But as I stared at the money and the hastily scrawled words, I felt something else, too—a grudging acknowledgment that at least he was trying to make amends.

MY MOTHER DROPPED me at my car an hour before I was due at the station, just enough time to run around the corner and deal with my phone issue. With mixed feelings, I used $285 of the cash Kenny had sent me to get my cell-phone turned back on.

Back in my car, I brought the cellphone to life and, the moment it powered up, the device started dinging and buzzing like a furious swarm of bees. Messages and texts flooded my screen, and I hesitated for a moment before diving in. The sheer volume of missed messages was overwhelming, but, with my phone now fully operational, I felt a renewed sense of confidence. My toolbelt for life was getting restocked.

Scanning the voicemails, I chose the one from Bridget first. It was from before she knew my phone had been turned off and I listened to the message twice just to hear her voice. She rarely called me and I kept every voicemail she sent so I could listen to it when I felt like I had called her too often but still wanted to hear her voice.

Next, the high-pitched, cracking voice of an elderly woman filled my car. "Is that you Penny? Penny? Hello? Hello? Penny, is that you?" She sounded both hopeful and confused.

I couldn't help but laugh as I deleted the message. The woman was a former patient of mine who kept calling me, mistaking me for someone named Penny. I had no idea who Penny was, but I hoped they were both doing well and that my former patient would hear from Penny soon.

My amusement at the Penny message quickly vanished as I pressed play on another voicemail, one from a blocked number.

The voice was eerie and haunting, clearly run through a scrambler to disguise the caller's identity. "Tonight they will capture the true Waxlace Strangler. I want you to be in Buck Lake Park at eight thirty."

I froze, staring at my phone, heart pounding in my chest. I checked the date and time the voicemail had been left. Four in the afternoon on the day of the murder.

Four and a half hours *before* Cara was killed.

My hands shook as I clutched my phone, my eyes darting around the parking lot. Paranoia gnawed at my insides and I instinctively locked the car doors.

The killer had tried to warn me. But why?

My first thought—after berating myself for not keeping my phone line working—was Jared.

When we'd met him in the library, he'd clearly thought he had a connection with me based on a single article I'd written two decades ago. *You're my only hope,* he'd said.

I couldn't wrap my head around it.

My next thought was: *Clint.*

I needed to share this with Clint and I called him at the office.

"Hello?" he said casually, picking up after two rings.

"Clint, are you in the office yet?"

"Yeah, we're all here." The lightness in his voice was jarringly out of touch with what I was feeling. "I was telling Maria about the sauce on that sea bass tartare. Wasn't it amazing how they infused that Meyer lemon with—"

"Clint, listen!"

He cleared his throat. "Okay? What's up?"

"I got a call from the killer. *Before* the murder. Just… just stay in the office. I'll be there in ten."

CHAPTER 16

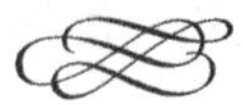

I FLUNG the door open and stumbled into the cramped WSP conference room. Carlo, Maria, and Clint were already there. Carlo and Maria were picking at their breakfast sandwiches with a casual indifference that seemed even more out of place than Clint's fawning description of the tartare.

I had this voicemail, potentially from the killer, and I needed them to hear it. "Guys," I gasped, gripping the back of a chair for support, "I just got this voicemail. You have to listen to it."

Carlo looked up from his sandwich, his green eyes narrowing with concern. "What is it, Macy?"

I fumbled with my phone, my fingers trembling as I hit play. The eerie, scrambled voice filled the room.

The message ended and a silence settled over us like a heavy blanket. Maria put her sandwich down, her face pale. "What *was* that, Macy?"

"I don't know," I admitted. "Sounds like he wanted us to stop the murder."

"Or catch the killer in the act," Clint said. "Play it again."

I played it again. Then again.

Clint leaned back in his chair, rubbing his temples. "Okay,

let's think this through. It could be the killer. Some people have trouble coming out from behind bars. Maybe it was Jared calling, hoping to get caught. Or maybe it's someone who knew the crime was going to happen and wanted us to have stopped it."

Carlo frowned, his eyes darting between the three of us. "But why would they contact you, Macy?"

"Right," Maria added. "That came *before* you had any connection to this case."

I shook my head, feeling a knot forming in my stomach. "Jared. I mean, it has to be Jared. My only connection to this comes from the original case, which I covered briefly." I shook my head. "Whoever it is, they've got my number, and they're playing some twisted game with us."

Maria's brow furrowed as she considered the possibilities. "What about Bob's nephew, Bob? Could he have gotten your number from Bob senior?"

"Maybe," I said. "While back, all the neighbors got together to strategize combating the modern day pirates. Even had a police officer—Lucy O' something or other—give a presentation. A phone tree was part of the strategy, so Bob's nephew might have gotten it there."

"Pirates?" Carlo asked.

"Yeah, shoreline houses up and down the peninsula have a lot of break-ins. The pirates escape on the Salish Sea," I informed the team.

"He also could have just looked it up online," Carlo pointed out.

"So we've got two things to figure out," Maria added, "who made the call, and where it came from."

Carlo's expression hardened. "Let's start with the call itself. Macy, can you play it again? Maybe we'll pick up on something we missed the first time."

I replayed the voicemail, and we listened intently, searching for clues in the scrambled voice.

When it ended, Maria spoke up, her voice hesitant. "So, the voice is run through a scrambler and—"

"Is it possible to somehow reverse-engineer the scrambling process?" I asked. "To identify the caller."

"I'll give it to Katya," Clint said. "It's not totally impossible, but depends on the sophistication of the scrambler technology, the signal quality, the amount of background noise, and the amount of computing power we have." He sighed. "Like I said, I'll give it to Katya, but we shouldn't expect much." Clint opened his eyes, a glimmer of hope in his gaze. "In the meantime, I'll call the judge and try to get a court order for the location of the call."

"That's amazing," I said. "You can do that?"

Carlo answered, "It's not as simple as tracing the call. For a voicemail, we need the phone company to dig up the records of when the call was made to your phone, and then find the location based on cellphone towers. It's not an easy get."

"But worth a try," Maria said.

Just as we were about to start making calls to organize our next steps, Clint's phone rang. He glanced at the screen, his eyebrows raised in surprise. "It's Laney, the library security agent," he said, putting the call on speakerphone.

"Hey, Laney," Clint greeted her, "you're on speaker with my team. What's up?"

"Clint, I've got some new information about the kid who was at the library on the night in question." Laney's voice was tense. "He came in to work today and said he doesn't actually remember if it was Jared or someone else who was there that night."

We exchanged worried glances. Maria frowned, her fingers tapping on the table. "Why would he say that *now*?"

Laney hesitated before continuing. "He told me he thinks he might've told the police officers what he thought they wanted to hear. He didn't want to disappoint them or cause any trouble."

Clint's jaw clenched, but he kept his voice steady. "Any idea why he'd be unsure of his own memory?"

Laney sighed. "Well, this kid's had a rough life. He's been homeless for a while, bouncing between shelters and friends' couches. Takes care of his sickly homeless mother. Sometimes he sleeps in the library when he can't find anywhere else to go. He's been trying to stay under the radar and avoid getting caught up in any trouble." She paused, her voice softening. "He's got a lot on his plate. He's been struggling to finish high school while working multiple jobs to make ends meet. He's a good kid, Clint, just... I don't know. You know how teenagers are."

As Laney spoke, a twinge of sympathy gripped my heart. Life had dealt this kid a difficult hand, and now he was caught up in a dangerous game that was entirely beyond his control.

Clint ran a hand through his hair, frustration etched on his face. "All right, Laney. Thanks for letting us know. We'll have to reevaluate our information and see what we can do. Before I let you go, what time do you open today?"

"Ten AM, why?"

"Jared hasn't been seen or heard from since yesterday. If he shows up there today, call me ASAP, okay?"

"Will do. Good luck, Clint," Laney said before hanging up.

We shared a long silence, each doing the same math in our head. The video footage of Jared had ended around 7 PM. The library worker had initially told police he'd seen Jared leaving at 8 PM. If he'd been wrong, if Jared had left an hour earlier, that gave him just enough time to catch a ferry to Hansville and kill Cara before returning home in time for his 10 PM digital curfew check in.

Carlo broke the silence. "There was a 7:35 ferry from Edmonds to Kingston."

"It's about fifteen miles north to the Edmonds ferry dock." I could fill in the details. "Can take between twenty and forty minutes to drive."

"How far from Kingston to the spot in Area One where the murder took place?" Maria asked.

"Fifteen minutes, if you drive like my mother, twenty or so if you drive by the posted speed limits," I said. "The timeline could work. Tight, but possible."

"Jared is back in the suspect lineup in a big way," Clint said.

Maria's eyes flicked between us, her mind clearly racing. "We've got to follow up on the voicemail. Here Macy, let me take your phone down the hall to Katya. She'll grab the meta-data, which we can give to the judge to try to force the cell carrier to give us a location."

I briefly considered my fourth amendment rights, but then thought of my own life and the life of a potential future victim.

I handed her my cell.

CHAPTER 17

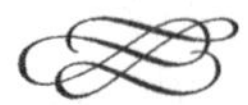

WHEN MARIA RETURNED from dropping off my phone, her face's usual confident glow had been replaced by a worried expression that looked jarring on her pleasant face. We looked up, our conversations coming to a halt as we waited for her to speak.

"Clint, Macy," she said, her voice unsteady, "Jacqueline wants to see you both. Now."

"Oh, a summons from the Iron Chief herself." Carlo was always quick with a quip, trying to bring some levity to the situation. "Good luck, you two. You're going to need it."

I shot Carlo a mock glare, but inside I felt a knot of anxiety tightening the muscles throughout my body. Jacqueline had a reputation for being tough and demanding, and her nickname wasn't just for show.

It had been some time since I'd been in trouble with a boss. The last time was when I was blamed for calling one of our hospital's frequent flyers "Duke Ding-Dong." He was an especially needy patient who used the call bell incessantly to assuage his cabin fever. I hadn't actually called him that—another nurse had—but I'd been happy to take the fall. I certainly laughed about it enough to deserve a reprimand.

Maria caught my eye, her lips curling into a teasing smile. "Hey, Macy, look at it this way: you're about to get hammered by the chief. That's like an initiation into the team."

I raised an eyebrow, my mind flashing back to my first encounter with Jacqueline. "You know, she already yelled at me about my dog on my first day here," I reminded them. What I didn't say was my real worry: that she'd found out about my suspended nursing license.

Carlo chuckled, his eyes dancing with amusement. "You've got a point there, Macy. But we all know Jacqueline's got more than one level of initiation. You're just moving up the ranks."

Maria nodded. "Carlo's right. We've all been there. It's practically a rite of passage."

"I think I've had enough hazing, thank you very much."

Clint, who had been silently observing the conversation, finally chimed in. "While I'm not exactly thrilled about facing Jacqueline either, we should probably get this over with. Who knows, maybe it's not as bad as we think."

As Clint and I finalized our plan and prepared to face the Chief, the knot of anxiety in my stomach tightened. It felt like I was walking into the lion's den. Turns out, I didn't like my place of employment to resemble a zoo any more than Chief Bangor did.

We entered her office, a space that felt like a different world compared to the stark, utilitarian conference room. The large room had a window looking out onto a majestic cedar tree. Everything was neat and clean, and a large framed photo of Chief Bangor at a Mariner's game with her uncle, the lieutenant governor of Washington State, hung prominently on the wall.

Chief Bangor stood behind her immaculate desk, her expression severe, her voice formal. "Sit," she commanded.

We obeyed without hesitation.

"So," she began icily, "tell me about your interview with Jared Norris yesterday."

Clint recounted our encounter at the library and as he spoke, I noticed that he avoided mentioning Jared's disappearance. Was he trying to protect us, or was he simply attempting to avoid more trouble? He also failed to mention the call I'd gotten.

"And what do you think is going on?" the Chief asked, her eyes narrowing.

Clint hesitated, and I decided to jump in. "We don't know, Chief. Jared is clearly disturbed and was previously convicted of murder, but we can't say for sure this time it's him."

Her face darkened, her anger simmering just below the surface. "Well, I just got off the phone with Seattle PD," she said, her voice rising. "And they're *furious*. They say you two scared away their guy." She raised a thin, well-manicured eyebrow. "Did you know he's missing?"

"I was about to get to that, Chief," Clint said.

"Now, they're pissed at *me*. I need *you* to tell *me* how you plan to iron out this issue. I will need the SPD when I run for state district attorney. Don't screw with this case, and don't screw with them. If you do, you'll be looking for new jobs. Perhaps you'll be in luck and the zoo will be hiring."

My anger flared, but I bit my tongue.

"We understand your concerns, Chief," Clint responded cautiously. "We did our interview and, well... I don't know what we could have done differently."

She glared at us, her frustration palpable. "I know you're both dedicated to this case, but I need you to understand the implications of your actions. I can't afford to have the Seattle PD doubting my leadership."

I couldn't hold back any longer. "With all due respect, Chief," I said, my voice strained, "we're not playing politics here. We're trying to solve a murder." All my years of patient advocacy translated well into victim advocacy. I was well aware of how the healthcare system could steamroll the needs of a patient or a nurse, and it was disheartening to see a similar dynamic coming from above in the justice system.

Chief Bangor's eyes flashed with anger, but Clint quickly stepped in. "We understand your position, Chief, and we'll be more careful in the future. We're gonna find Jared and solve this thing."

For a moment, it seemed as though our words had only fueled her anger. But then she exhaled slowly, her shoulders slumping ever so slightly. "Fine," she said, her tone still tense. "But I'm counting on you both to get this case solved, quickly and quietly." She leaned forward, her eyes glancing at me, then locking onto Clint. "I'm giving you both forty-eight hours to bring this case to a conclusion," she said, her voice hard as steel. "If you don't, I'm handing it over to the FBI."

Clint's eyes widened, and he immediately objected. "You can't do that!"

"I can, and I will," she snapped. "I don't owe you an explanation, but the FBI can take any serial killer case they want. If I tell them we think the Waxlace Strangler is back, it's on their plate, not yours. For now, officially, it's a separate case. But I can change that anytime I want."

Her gaze shifted to me, and I could feel the weight of her scrutiny. "And why, exactly, is Macy still on this case?"

Clint didn't hesitate in his response. "*Still*? We just hired her! She's smart and knows the Waxlace Strangler case. She... she got a call from..." He trailed off.

"A call from who?"

"We don't know for sure. Someone warned her about the murder. *Before* it occurred."

Chief Bangor held up her hands, silencing him. "Don't say any more." She paced for a moment, then stared out the window. Not facing us, she said, "I should send this thing to the Feds right now but... damn it would look good if we solved it ourselves." She turned, having made up her mind. "Forty-eight hours," she said. "Get me something in the next forty-eight."

I could see Clint's fists clench as he mulled over her words.

"If I don't see progress, and soon, I won't hesitate to bring in the big guns," she warned.

Clint and I left her office.

My mind raced with the urgency of our situation.

Clocks were ticking, and no one wanted to see time run out.

CHAPTER 18

BACK IN THE CONFERENCE ROOM, we found Carlo and Maria standing close together, looking lost in their own world. They didn't notice us walk in.

Carlo gave Maria a sly wink and she rolled her eyes before saying, "You know, you'd be perfect for a friend of mine."

"Oh really, a *friend*, huh?" he replied, a playful smile tugging at the corner of his mouth. "Fine with me." He looked away from her, feigning disinterest. "I would probably like your friend *way* better than I like you."

Maria smirked, "I guess I'd better show you back to my friend zone, then."

Carlo feigned a pout. "Nooo, I like the zone I'm in," he whined.

The two looked so similar, at first I'd thought it could be a Luke and Leia situation. Now I was sure it was actually a Leia and Han Solo dynamic.

Maria caught sight of us, and she turned, her eyes widening in surprise. "We were just discussing that, umm, that voicemail on Macy's phone," she said, trying to sound casual.

Clint raised an eyebrow, not buying her weakly executed cover-up.

"How'd it go with the Chief?" Carlo asked. "Did the bullets clear your major organs?"

"We're fine," I responded. "Clean exit wounds."

"What's the word on the voicemail, then?" Clint jumped back in to work on the case.

"We requested the court order to trace the location of the call while you were away, but that'll be a day, minimum, and that's if the carrier cooperates right away." Maria glanced at Carlo, and gave him an encouraging nod.

Carlo said, "But we think we found something else."

I felt a pang of jealousy as I watched them working so seamlessly together. Their connection was palpable, and sweet. I missed having a person. I pushed the feeling aside and returned my focus to the case.

"What is it?" Clint asked.

"Katya was able to isolate some of the background noise in the call," Carlo said. He pressed play on his laptop. The scrambled voice had been turned down somehow, the background noise amplified. I heard clanging dishes and murmuring voices.

"Okay," I said, "but—"

"Wait for it," Maria said.

Then I heard it. "'Athenian Scramble, hold the spinach, extra feta, rye toast.'" The voice was deep and partially scrambled, similar to the original call, but the words were unmistakable.

"What the hell was that?" Clint asked.

"Unless we're wrong," Carlo said, "which we're not, the call came from Apollo's Diner in Seattle. Looked up their menu online. The dish matches their signature breakfast scramble. Feta, spinach, tomato, black olives, three eggs, and—"

"They don't need the recipe," Maria said.

Clint nodded, his brow furrowed in thought. "Good work,

you two. But the call showed up as a private number on Macy's cell. Why would a diner have a blocked number?"

"It doesn't," Carlo said.

"Let him finish," Maria added.

Carlo stood and walked to the whiteboard. "We think the call Macy got was from a cellphone in the diner. But we also looked through the 911 calls from that day. Found a call from the same diner, but from their landline. Made just ten minutes *after* the call to Macy's phone."

"Wait wait wait," Clint said. "Someone called Macy's cell from their cell. Then called the Kitsap police from the landline of the restaurant?"

Carlo and Maria nodded in unison.

I asked, "You think it was the same person?"

"Whether the same person or two people working together," Maria said, "we either have our guy, or someone who knew about our guy's plans in advance."

Clint nodded. "And did you—"

"Speak with Daniels?" Carlo asked. "Yes."

"Who's Daniels?" I asked.

"Kitsap Sheriff. We have a lot of overlapping jurisdiction."

Maria shook her head. "He said they sent a patrol out to Buck Lake that night after they got the call. Didn't see a damn thing."

Carlo looked furious. "They left the scene thinking it was a prank call."

I shook my head. Police had been at the scene of the crime, were warned of the murder before it occurred, and somehow they'd missed it.

Clint must've read my face. "It's a massive park," he explained. "Trails everywhere, the lake itself." He sighed. "Not like they have twenty extra guys around to run down every tip."

"We're looking into why we didn't get the information about the 911 call sooner," Carlo said.

"Probably too embarrassed to admit it," Maria said.

"Anyway," Carlo continued, "we got a hold of someone at the diner in Seattle. Didn't get far. No one there remembers anything unusual happening. But the owner *did* say they often let people use their phone, and they have twenty staff members in total. It could have been anyone."

Clint glanced at me. "We will head to the diner after this, but first, Maria, what about Bob? Update me on your progress on the Bob angle."

"Yes," Maria began. "Did some public records searches and we found the nephew, Robert Dalton. He does live in Iowa, like he told Macy. Haven't been able to reach him or get flight info yet. We did find a flight he *could have* taken. If he'd heard about his uncle in the middle of the night and taken the first flight, timing could work."

"In the meantime," Carlo added, "we're in the process of securing a warrant to delve into various records, financial transactions, and phone calls. Figure out if he was in town when he wasn't supposed to be."

Clint tapped a pen on the table. "Good."

"There's one more thing we found," Maria continued. "We think the murder was random."

"How do we know that?" Clint asked.

"Carlo, I can't," Maria said. "You say it."

"Search team found Cara's phone at the lake," Carlo said, his voice taking on a somber tone. "She'd taken multiple pictures of herself meant for her Instagram account. None of them sent. No cell service so far outside of town."

"Looked like a beautiful night," Maria said. "Until all that happened to her... well until what happened, happened."

That bastard. The nagging fear that it could have been any girl, that it could have easily been Bridget who was killed. I didn't want to imagine it.

I glanced at the clock on the wall, acutely aware of the

ticking minutes. We had less than 48 hours to bring this case to a close if we wanted to keep our jobs.

And, if the killer planned to strike again, we needed to act fast in order to save another young girl's life.

Then I remembered something. "Clint, on the way to the ferry, can we stop in Kingston?"

He stood and headed for the door. "It's closer to take the Bremerton boat, but why?"

"I might have more documents on the case."

CHAPTER 19

In the matching SUV behind us, Carlo and Maria seemed to be arguing, though it was hard to see through the tinted glass.

I glanced at Clint and asked, "Are they really just colleagues? They argue like an old married couple."

Clint shrugged. "Who knows with people?"

Carlo and Maria took the State Route 3 North onramp and Clint and I headed south.

Clint explained that Carlo and Maria would be taking the Bremerton Ferry straight into Seattle. They were headed to the records office for the Seattle PD to try to see if the wax in the original case matched the wax from the current case. "Not everything from back then has become electronic," he added.

Clint and I arrived at the storage unit and I pulled out the copy of the storage key Kenny had made for me years ago. The top of the key was diamond-shaped and painted with enamel to look like the cartoon version of a diamond. He knew how forgetful I was and how much difficulty I had telling one key from another. So, he'd had it made special *for when you need to unlock a storage unit full of your precious gems and jewelry.*

Kenny was a real piece of work, but he did have his moments.

I breathed a sigh of relief when I saw that, to my surprise, the only lock on the storage door was the one Kenny had placed. Not only had they not evicted us, they hadn't locked our unit for non-payment, thank goodness.

I bent down, my feet shifting unpredictably over gravel that had spilled up onto the concrete pad that was the floor of the unit. The door lifted from the bottom and slid up easily until it reached my knees. It caught halfway up, jolting my arm and releasing the smashing sound of metal on metal.

I could feel the weight of something heavy pushing against the door from inside. I hesitated, then shoved the door with all my strength. The door groaned and then shot open with a *clang clang clang*. As I continued to lift, I shoved a box that threatened to spill its contents when the door was no longer blocking it from falling. The box went crashing away from me into the bowels of the junk cache.

There were those *stupid* leather seats Kenny had bought and some boxes I didn't recognize that seemed to be full of car parts and other miscellaneous debris Kenny had hastefully shoved into the unit. The place smelled just like the Wrench King. *Gah!*

Precious gems and jewelry, my ass.

"Damn it, Kenny," I muttered under my breath. I imagined the shrapnel from my brain exploding and deeply embedding itself in his flesh. He wouldn't know what hit him.

I stood on my tiptoes and, using my cell phone flashlight, scanned the contents from above. I wasn't tall enough to see very deeply into the pile.

"How can I help?" Clint came alongside me and shone his flashlight into the abyss of the storage unit as well. He was taller, so had a better angle than I.

"It's a white box with red lines," I said. "And it says *Mac's papers* on the top and all the sides… I think. Maybe *Mac's stuff.*

Could be just *Mac*. This hellhole is mostly my ex's stuff and he didn't label anything." Kenny could never keep The Wrench King organized, and when he couldn't find a tool, he'd buy a new one. Once he borrowed some of my dad's tools and that was a disaster. I don't know who called me more that year, our creditors or my dad trying to get his tools back. My father never saw those tools again.

Our flashlights drew circles on the metal side walls and cement back wall and seemed to blink off and on as we scanned the dark reaches of the unit.

Just as I was about to start climbing over the pile of leather seats, Clint pointed towards the ground right in front of us. "This it?" he asked.

"Damn it, Kenny." I felt my body melt into the shape of the wilted box that sat crushed underneath two white leather Audi seats. The seats were balanced precariously, one turned upside down on the other. I kicked my foot against the seats and tried to pull the box out from underneath it. My impatience was getting the better of me.

"Let me help," Clint offered. I stood aside as he lifted the seats, allowing me to grab the crushed box from underneath.

I hoped he didn't see my blush at the sight of him engaging his strength. Watching men lift heavy things is my kryptonite.

I balanced the flattened lid over the top of the box and tucked it underneath my left arm. Clint closed the door and replaced the lock then handed me the key.

"I'm never going in there again," I promised myself.

"I wouldn't if I were you," Clint agreed. "Though you might want to sell all those seats. Still good as new and they're worth real money."

Real money or no, never seeing those seats again would be worth more to me than whatever they might sell for.

As the ferry chugged along, I opened up the box of old documents, finding lots of dead ends. Notes for stories I pursued but never wrote, pages of doodles, a letter I'd written to Kenny and never sent, even my high school diploma.

But under stacks of distractions, I found what I was looking for. A simple manila folder, given to me by a young officer who didn't believe Jared was guilty and wanted to get the word out in the press. It was possible he was trying to sleep with me because, when he found out I was married, he dried up as a source.

Either way, inside the folder were dozens of badly photocopied crime scene photos from the original case, ones I didn't think Clint had seen yet.

I handed him the file just as I received a text from Bridget. She wanted the recipe for blueberry coffee cake for a brunch she was attending on Saturday. I shot back a message that I would send it when I got home later that night. She had asked me for this recipe three times this year. I made a mental note to gift her a recipe box.

Turning back to the photos, I quickly found something intriguing. There was a picture of Jared and it looked like he was wearing some kind of brace or cast on his wrist. Depending on when this picture was taken, could he have wrestled with a young girl and pulled the wax laces tight enough to strangle someone with a busted wrist? I shared my observation with Clint, who remained unconvinced by this "evidence."

I had to admit, even to myself, it wasn't much of a lead. The evidence pointing to Jared as the killer was simply too much to ignore. But as we continued poring over the documents, a nagging feeling in the back of my mind pulled at me.

There was something more we needed to uncover.

CHAPTER 20

He stalks the streets, unable to silence the thoughts swirling in his head. Meds, poison, control... a cacophony of disjointed ideas battling for dominance.

Rain pours down.

Hunger. He feels hunger.

Thoughts, squirming and writhing in his mind, become a tangled knot.

The meds, has he taken them? He doesn't think he has. Are they trying to poison him, control him, a puppet hanging from their strings, or is he a balloon held by a single detached string, on his own with only the wind influencing his dance.

His plan, his precious plan, not working, never working. Why doesn't she do what he wants, what he expects? He thinks she believes him. Confusion, frustration, a burning mind ember.

The alley calls him, water splashes, the puddles dance.

In the alley, he stops, everything becoming clear all at once. A dumpster waits, a bird pecks, soggy popcorn its treasure. He speaks to the bird, his words spilling out, a torrent. He knows, deep down, that the bird will not talk back, but it doesn't matter. It's a connection, a sweet connection.

A lifeline.

Everything clicks into place.

The popcorn.

Food, too, is a lifeline.

He is hungry.

It is raining and he is hungry.

Has he taken his meds?

Has he eaten?

He remembers he is marching to get food, so he marches on. The city's cold gaze is suffocating. The buildings are watchful sentinels, their eyes the only objective observer. He stops again as the buildings close in around him. He tries to breathe, his lungs expanding against the side walls of the tall structures, but their weight is crushing. More of the sky is swallowed with every exhale.

The rain drums on, an arrhythmic heartbeat, a cadence mirroring his thoughts, scattered and frenzied.

Graffiti colors sing to him, sirens wail, the scent of rain and decay a perfume that clings to his skin. They merge into one sense—sight, sound, feel, smell, and taste. He tries to separate his senses and anchor each one like strings tied to balloons. He will use the strings to tether himself to reality. Reality is himself as a young boy, the handful of strings clenched in his fist and he'd better not let go. But reality is elusive and the strings are slipping from his grasp.

He will go to the diner for food.

He can feel his heart pounding in his chest, the blood coursing through his veins, a reminder that he is alive, even as his mind splinters. He tries to hold on to the fragments, to piece them back together, but pieces are missing.

He thinks himself innocent. He is in desperate need of order, justice, revenge, in the very least comprehension.

The rain falls, but can't wash away a thing.

The diner is a beacon.

CHAPTER 21

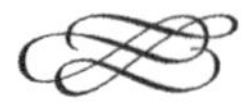

CLINT and I stepped into Apollo's Famous Diner, a bustling hive of activity in the heart of Seattle. The place was alive with the clanging of dishes, the chatter of patrons. The crowd was a mix of old-timers hunched over their newspapers and young professionals grabbing a quick lunch, all seeking warmth and comfort.

We were there to speak with the owner.

I turned to Clint. "Should we show him the picture of Jared first?" I asked.

"Your instincts are spot on," Clint replied. "However, it's best not to influence a potential witness too early. In a court, a witness confidently stating, 'I know exactly who made that phone call,' holds more weight than if we were to show him a picture and inquire if it matches the caller's identity. Besides, who knows, it might have been the owner who made the call. We just have to see what he has to say first."

"That makes sense," I said.

And it did. Police interviews and nurse interviews were similar: asking open ended questions tended to get you more accurate answers than asking leading ones.

A waitress with a name tag that read "Sandy" caught our eye

and gestured for us to follow her towards the back when Clint introduced us. We wove our way through the maze of tables, and constant hum of conversation.

She led us to the owner, a bearded man who introduced himself as Apollo. He stood unusually upright, as though he had a steel bar holding him up and tethering him to the ceiling. Or maybe I was just slouching.

Following Apollo through the kitchen, we stopped in a cramped storage room stacked high with bags of rice, jars of sauce, and various dry goods. I let the scent of the bacon, oregano, and caramelized garlic fill my nostrils as I surveyed the organized chaos around us.

I glanced at Clint, who wasted no time in getting to the point. "Apollo, we're looking for a man believed to be a murderer who may have used your phone a few nights ago."

"I let lots of people use my phone." Apollo frowned, crossing his arms over his broad chest. "Every Tuesday and Friday, between noon and two, I routinely give away meals. You know, just before we get the new shipments in, to make space in the fridge. Homeless come around then and other times too."

"Do they use the phone?" Clint pressed.

"Sure. Sure. I let them use the cordless phone anytime out back in the alley under the awning." Apollo pointed toward the back of the building. "I keep the charger just inside the back door. They pass the phone around until the battery runs out, then switch it with one that's fully charged. Not like they've got a payphone they can use anymore, am I right?"

I glanced at Clint. "Well, there are still a few."

"Still, sometimes they're out there making calls late into the evening," Apollo continued. "They take messages if someone calls, and tell people what's on the menu. They know what to say. *'Thank you for calling Apollo's Famous Diner, how can I help you?'* Just like that. It's like I got an answering service. Saves me a bundle. I don't have to pay a hostess for a few hours, and I don't have to answer the phone myself. For some of them it gives them purpose, they earn their meal. For others a phone call to a family member is the highlight of their day."

His words struck me as sincere and honest. It was evident he genuinely cared for the people he helped.

As we continued to talk, Apollo was interrupted a couple of times by cooks asking questions about various recipes. He answered them with a patience that spoke volumes about his character.

As Clint asked a couple follow ups about the people who came in during the free sandwich hours, I began wondering if I was hungry. Being bombarded by the smells from the kitchen was taking its toll. I thought about bringing something from the diner home, to eat later that night. I thought of Gonzo's perpetually trembling body sidling up to my foil container of take-out food. Watching me remove the plastic lid, he would await small tidbits of the feta cheese that I would feed him by hand.

I smiled, feeling a pang of longing for Gonzo's company. I wondered if I would be able to break his *eating-on-the-table* routine. Likely not any time soon. Definitely not soon enough for my mother.

"Have you seen anyone suspicious lately?" Clint pressed.

"No idea, man." Apollo scratched his beard, pondering the question. "Like I said, people use the phone free range, like the chicken I serve. I couldn't tell you what anybody talks about on the phone out there anyway. Too busy running this place."

I didn't like the hard edge Clint was taking with Apollo. It seemed unnecessary, especially considering how friendly and helpful the diner owner had been so far. I didn't have experience being a detective, but I'd had plenty of experience interviewing people who were lying to me. Hell, as a nurse I'd probably interviewed more liars than Clint. Only difference being, my liars fibbed about *how-many-too-many* tylenol they were taking, or how the tylenol was actually oxycodone left over from their mother's hip surgery from five years ago.

"Apollo, how long have you had this diner?" I asked, trying to lighten the mood a bit.

"I took it over from my uncle about twenty years ago." He seemed pleased by the question. "I've been working here since I was a kid, starting with washing dishes."

"Wow, that's quite a journey," I said. "So, what are your top dishes here?"

Apollo rubbed his chin thoughtfully. "Well, we've got a mix of American stuff and Greek classics. But our burgers are pretty popular at lunch. You should try the 'Zeus' sometime. It's got two beef patties, gyro meat, feta cheese, tzatziki sauce, lettuce, tomato, and onion. It's a monster."

I could feel my stomach rumble as he described it.

"We've got a breakfast menu that will curl your taste buds, too," he continued. "We serve it all day. The Athenian omelet is a favorite—spinach, tomatoes, onions, Kalamata olives, and feta again. Comes with a side of hash browns or home fries and toast."

"You're making me hungry," I said.

I caught an annoyed glance from Clint, but I was trying to soften the guy up.

"We've got moussaka, pastitsio, and a bunch of souvlaki platters." Apollo didn't miss a beat as he went on. "Oh, and our spanakopita—you gotta try that. And for dessert, our homemade baklava, of course."

My mouth watered.

"I can see why this place is always busy," I said.

A rueful smile tugged at the corners of his lips. "Wish I could tell you who the guy was who made the call." He shook his head. "I can barely remember what day it is, let alone who might have made a call a few days ago."

It was a fair point. Running a busy diner was no small feat, and I knew Apollo had plenty on his plate.

Apollo tapped his watch and inched toward the door. "Listen folks, can we wrap this up here? I want to help but I've got to get this place ready for the next rush and then dinner service." He wiped his brow with the back of his forearm. "Takes a lot to keep this place afloat, you know."

Clint pulled out his phone. "One more thing. Do you recognize him?" He held it up, displaying a picture of Jared, his lean, gaunt face staring back at us.

Apollo's eyes widened in recognition, "Sure, I do." He nodded. "That's Jared. For the last year, he's been coming around here. And often."

The revelation sent a shiver down my spine.

"What does he usually order?" Clint asked.

"Does he talk to anyone?" I added.

"Have you noticed anything strange or different about him lately?" Clint continued, not giving Apollo time to answer.

The diner owner held up both hands. "Whoa whoa whoa. Strange? I might not know how to describe him any other way. Always with the dill pickles on his Reuben." He shook his head. "But, yeah, orders the same every time: Reuben, add pickles, with a side of coleslaw and an Arnold Palmer. I know people's orders just like *that*." He snapped his fingers.

"Anything else you can tell us about him?" Clint asked.

"He doesn't talk much. Mostly keeps to himself. Seen him talking to pigeons a few times out back." Apollo scratched his head, thinking hard. "The guy's always on edge though."

"How so?" Clint asked.

"Can't really say," Apollo said. "It's like he's waiting for something bad to happen. Something terrible."

CHAPTER 22

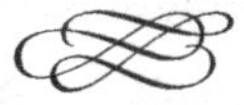

BIRDS CAN'T TALK back to him.

But then again, there *was* that crow. His only friend when they locked him away.

Rain, rain. Splash, splash.

And the diner. Where is the diner?

Was the crow whispering sweet lies through the window all those years?

Whispers about Heath?

Where was that window? The prison? His mind? Is the shadow a crow? Is the shadow a person? A whispering bird shadow. An audible machination of light?

Questions, doubts, swirling, skating grooves and divots in his muddled thoughts. Time for the Zamboni to smooth the ice.

The name Heath sieves through, a ghostly whisper, no longer a tantalizing enigma.

It matters where the skates are.

Doesn't matter. Never mind. What is mind is matter.

Out of the alley, he goes. Is it stomach or mind that his hunger gnaws? Never matter. No mind.

The diner beckons.

The diner beckons.

What beckons counts, and not the clicking latch behind you.

Hunger.

The splash of water from a passing car might melt his bones. The corner turned. The sign of the diner, neon flickering, casts a pale glow on the wet pavement.

He squints through the window. Safety is on the other side, a portal to warmth, to food, to life, to clarity of mind.

But, he needs to consider the devil he knows versus the other familiar devil.

Should he go in? Should he not?

Those calls, the bird calls that didn't work. He made two calls.

Trepidation, a trembling in his heart, a dance between hunger and danger.

Some birds are caged and some dirty birds are not. There but for the grace of God goes Heath.

Freedom is a state of mind. Both are lost.

The memories swirl, like birds caught in a whirlwind.

The prison cell, the crow, what Heath did.

The phone calls. The plan that went awry, the plan that leaves him here, adrift in this storm of confusion.

What should he do? What *can* he do? Who might he call now?

The current is too strong, too powerful, and it threatens to sweep him away. And yet, amid the chaos, a single, unwavering thought emerges:

Apollo's. His lighthouse. A Point No Point. A Reuben, add pickles.

He clings to the thought of his sandwich, a desperate hope that it will guide him through the darkness. Food is his lighthouse.

Sandwich, sandwich everywhere, but it's a dangerous crumb to eat.

He mustn't think.

He must only do.

CHAPTER 23

"DID JARED MAKE A CALL THAT NIGHT?" Clint asked Apollo.

"Like I said, everybody's using that phone." Apollo shrugged, looking genuinely apologetic. "I want to help, I really do, but you can see how busy this place is. I can't keep track of every call or everyone who comes in. I could have been in the kitchen preparing his Reuben sandwich while he was out back on the phone."

A loud crash came from the main restaurant area. Sounded like a tray of dishes hitting the floor. We all froze for a moment before Apollo hurried away to handle the situation, concern etched on his face.

Clint and I followed him back into the dining room, where the staff scrambled to clean up the mess. I stared through the big window out onto the street. The rain was still coming down, washing away the grime of the city, but not my unease. We knew the call had come from this diner, and that it was probably Jared who'd made it, but no one knew where Jared was.

I was about to ask Clint to try the SPD again, to find out if anyone had gotten a lead on our suspect, when I saw him.

Out the window, wild eyes staring in at us, rain dripping

from his gaunt face, still wearing the same creepy white on white on white he had been wearing at the library: it was Jared.

Had he been outside all night? Was that why he'd missed his curfew?

"There he is, Clint." I tapped Clint on the shoulder and pointed. "It's Jared, standing right there, in the rain."

When he recognized us, his eyes went wide with a mixture of fear and desperation, making him look like a half-starved wild animal caught in a trap. His unkempt hair was plastered to his forehead and he was shivering, but it was clear that the cold was the least of his worries.

Clint burst out of the diner and into the rain. I was right behind him, leaping over and sometimes splashing in the puddles as I tried to keep up.

With his head start, Jared was twenty or thirty yards ahead of Clint, and I was quite a ways behind him, which was fine by me. I might have been tough, but I wasn't a cop, and I wasn't trained for this kind of pursuit.

The rain beat down on me as I ran, soaking through my clothes. The city's soundscape was muffled by the downpour, the sirens and hum of traffic distant and surreal.

Jared had taken off at a sprint—his speed a surprise—but managed to make it only a block and a half before his body gave out. Collapsing onto the wet pavement, he gasped for breath as his frame convulsed. It was a pitiful sight. Laying there half submerged in a puddle, his hands up in a submissive gesture, he looked as though he might have a heart attack at any moment.

Clint reached him first, his movements swift and decisive as he secured handcuffs around Jared's trembling wrists. When I finally caught up, my lungs were burning, my heart pounding in my chest. The rain did not relent. I shivered as it continued to pour down on us.

I had only been in the rain for a few minutes. And even that had me missing the Olympic Rain Shadow that protects Hansville from some of the forty inches of rain Seattle gets each year. Living at the edge of nowhere did have *some* advantages. But who knew how long Jared had been out in it and how long it had been since his last meal. I was in bad shape but Jared looked to be in *really* bad shape.

"My meds," Jared wheezed, his voice barely audible above the rain. "If you're gonna arrest me, I need my meds. And my Reuben."

THE INTERROGATION ROOM at the WSP offices was small and smelled like newly applied concentrated Pine Sol, which made me wonder what had happened in this room the last time it had been used.

We'd grabbed some food from the diner after the arrest, both because we needed it and because Jared looked like he might pass out from hunger at any minute.

Now, Clint was ready to begin questioning Jared, who sat across from us, crossing and uncrossing his legs and looking even more gaunt and deranged under the harsh lighting.

"So, Jared Norris," Clint began. "We have a lot to discuss. I guess I'll start with the big one. How'd you do it? How'd you manage to get from the library to the forest at Buck Lake so—"

Jared let out a strange sound, somewhere between a growl and a whimper. He opened his mouth like he wanted to speak.

Clint and I watched him. I don't know what my partner was thinking, but I was curious what Jared would say, and was happy to let him lead the way.

"Heath," Jared babbled, his voice a hoarse whisper, "Heath. He whispered through the crow, the bird spoke the truth, only the birds speak truth, but it slithered and writhed. Macy, you knew,

Macy, I thought you knew." The fluorescent light above flickered occasionally, casting an unsettling glow over the space. "The birds were tucked under your wings and you were their only hope, the salvation. But the darkness, it swallows and consumes, and the birds, they chatter and sing, they can only fly when they need to run. They can't fly through bars. Can't you hear them Macy?"

As I watched Jared, I felt a mix of shock and sadness wash over me. This man was clearly disturbed. His words were a tangled mess of frayed thoughts and delusions, much less coherent than when we'd interviewed him in the library.

And yet, at the same time, he seemed to be *trying* to tell us something.

"Can't fly through bars, can they, Macy? No one can..." For the next five minutes, his monologue continued, a stream-of-consciousness ramble that twisted and turned like a labyrinth. It was as if I was witnessing a strange amalgamation of James Joyce and Gollum. I was captivated and horrified, trying to find meaning in his words while also trying to figure out what was going on in his mind.

Eventually, Jared's energy waned and he slumped in his chair, his chest heaving as he struggled to catch his breath.

Clint seized the opportunity to interject. "Did you call Macy and the Kitsap Sheriff's office last Tuesday, warning of the murder near Buck Lake?"

Jared mumbled something incoherent, his eyes vacant and unfocused.

Clint pressed on, determined to get answers. "Why did you kill Cara? Why did you come to Hansville to strangle an innocent girl? Was it because you were locked up for twenty years, unable to kill, trained every day NOT to kill, and you just couldn't keep yourself from doing it?"

Again, Jared's response was a garbled, unintelligible mumble. Something about birds with a sprinkling of me being his only hope. Where had he gotten the idea that I was his Obi-Wan Kenobi?

I placed a hand on Clint's shoulder, urging him to calm down. I could tell that his frustration was mounting, but I knew we weren't going to get anywhere by pushing Jared too hard.

I decided to take the lead. "Jared, I need to know how I can help you."

"Yes. Yes," Jared said. "Please help me. I'm your little bird."

"Why did you call me?" I asked, locking eyes with Jared. There was a glimmer of recognition in his gaze. "Was it because of the story I wrote way back then? You wanted me to know another girl was going to die?"

He nodded weakly, and I felt a strange mixture of relief and unease.

"I really don't know anything, Jared." I sighed. "Back then, I had a source in the police who thought you might be innocent, and I printed that. That's all."

He sat up straight, his chest puffed out. "I *am* innocent." Just like that, he collapsed again, head in his hands. "The birds know. *You* know."

"No, I *don't* know Jared. And right now, you look pretty guilty." I hesitated for a moment, waiting for him to look back up. When he did, tears rolled down his cheeks. I searched his face for any sign of understanding. "I need your help, Jared. I need you to tell us what happened."

Jared's eyes darted around the room, as if he were only now realizing where he was. A brief moment of clarity seemed to wash over him, and his gaze settled back on me. "Okay," he said, his voice a low hiss of pain, "I'll tell you everything."

CHAPTER 24

"It was... the birds," Jared murmured, his voice trembling. He paused and looked up as though that was a sufficient explanation.

"What did the birds do?" I asked.

"They whispered secrets, terrible secrets, and I couldn't..." Jared wiped his face with his pale, near-skeletal hands. His words were slow and hesitant, like he was trying to piece together the fragments of his shattered mind. "I couldn't ignore them."

I wanted to pellet him with questions, but I could tell he was ready to keep going.

Clint looked ready to pounce as well, and I wondered how long he could contain himself. He released his grip on the table and sat back in his chair, letting the information come to him instead of fighting to go after it.

As Jared continued, the tiny room disappeared around me and I felt as though I could have been anywhere, like I was sucked into Jared's world, his mind, and it was the only thing that existed.

"The birds told me about Heath, the man who orchestrated it

all. He was the one all along. The one on the ice. And then... then the darkness came," he whispered. "I tried to resist, I tried so hard. But it was... it was too strong, and I couldn't... I couldn't fight it."

"But why, Jared?" I pleaded with him, my voice a mix of desperation and compassion. "Why Cara? What did she have to do with any of this?"

Jared's eyes clouded over with tears and, for a moment, he seemed lost in his own pain. "I don't know," he finally admitted. "I don't know why it had to be her. She was there. Wrong time at the right place. But I tried to tell you. They were supposed to save her."

His words hung in the air, heavy with sorrow and regret.

I looked at Clint, who seemed just as shaken as I was. This was closer to an admission of guilt than either of us thought we'd get. He'd just admitted to making the warning call, and I was beginning to think that "Heath" might be another part of Jared, a split-off, fragmented part of his personality he tried to fight, tried to hold down.

"Did you drag Cara from the lake back into the woods?" Clint asked. "Back into Area One?"

"*I*?" Jared spat, his whole demeanor changing from broken dove to enraged eagle. "*I* did nothing." Jared's eyes filled with a mix of hope and desperation as he continued, the words tumbling out of him like water from a dam that had finally burst. "The police all those years ago, they got it all wrong. They didn't listen to me... like you're not listening to me now."

"*We* are here now," Clint offered, "and we *are* listening."

"Right," I agreed. "We're listening."

"No, *you* don't listen." He shot an accusatory glance at Clint. "But I think you will, Macy." He looked at me, his gaze imploring. "I believe you'll believe me."

During my nursing school rounds at a psychiatric facility, I encountered a man with schizoaffective disorder. When I first met him, I thought, *what the heck is this guy doing here? He isn't sick at all.*

Then I experienced him when he was symptomatic.

He had delusions, hallucinations, posturing behaviors, and fluctuating emotions. He legit belonged in the institution. But he would occasionally shift to a stable mental state, like he had the first time I met him. It would happen randomly, regardless of when he had last taken his medications. In those clear moments, he engaged in small talk, shared stories about his children, academic pursuits, and regrets of being unable to consistently support his family due to his illness. I later learned moments of clarity were common in schizophrenic disorders.

It felt as though Jared were switching into a lucid state similar to my experience years ago with this man. He had been suffering and then was abruptly alleviated as though his mind had made a choice to allow him a moment of respite from the disease.

I nodded repeatedly, trying to encourage Jared as he went on, his voice low and urgent.

"Those shoelaces... yes, they had my blood on them, but it wasn't because I strangled anyone. The laces came from the skates I always borrowed from the ice rink. I always borrowed the same pair of skates. All the other ones weren't worn in, and they hurt my feet. So, I always used the same old ones. The teal and green 44s."

He paused, searching for the words, his desperation palpable. "The blood on the laces, it wasn't from my fingers bleeding from pulling the laces to strangle someone. It was from taking a bad fall two weeks before… before the first girl. Some of the blood must have ended up on my laces after the fall. I didn't strangle someone. It was just my blood on the laces. I still have a scar from when I busted my wrist on the ice."

He pointed at his wrist, where a faded pink gash was evident.

I was reminded of the photo I showed Clint earlier and glanced over at him. He seemed to be wrestling with Jared's explanation.

Turning my attention back to Jared, I said, "Why didn't you tell the police this back then?" I asked softly, trying to reconcile the man before me with the monster I was no longer so sure I should believe him to be.

He shook his head, his eyes welling up with tears. "I tried, Macy. I tried so hard to tell them. Sometimes they had me on the pills, so many pills, and I couldn't speak for myself. And the girls, all of them, came to the rink. I'd seen them, talked to them. They knew I knew them. Sometimes I was too ill and my words wouldn't come out straight. Sometimes they just laughed and told me I was a liar. They wanted someone to blame. Once they had me, they locked me into the dovecote."

"Dovecote?" I asked.

"House for doves or pigeons," Clint said, "like a dog kennel but for birds."

I was trying to reconcile this new information with what I knew about the case.

"The calluses on your fingers that matched the laces?" Clint added, his voice hard.

Jared didn't waver, continuing to explain his side of the story. "Those were calluses from pulling my laces tight. Every serious skater has those."

"We have one lace, but where are these skates now?" Clint pressed.

Jared shrugged.

"But Jared, there was footage of you stealing the skates from the skate rink," I said. "Where are the skates now?"

"I don't know." Jared's eyes began to well up. "I tried to find the skates for the police but they were gone." His voice heightened, tinged with notes of desperation. "I could never skate again. One, because no other ice skates would fit me just right, I couldn't get comfortable in any other skates. And two, because they sent me to the dovecote for twenty years."

As he spoke, a new burst of tears began to stream down his face. "I just want my skates," he sobbed. "Why did Heath have to take them? I think he took them, I know he took them. He could've left the skates and just taken the lace. I could get new laces for the skates, but I'll never be able to replace those skates."

His words were filled with an almost manic desperation. His speech was more coherent than it had been at the beginning of the interview, but his anguish was more palpable. And despite his disturbed mental state, there was a sincerity in Jared's words that I couldn't ignore.

My internal monologue raced, trying to process everything he'd said. Could he really be innocent? And, if so, how did he know to call me to warn me about the murder?

I reached out a hand to console him. "We want to help you find the skates," I told him gently.

Clint nodded, his own expression softening. "We'll look into what you've said, Jared. We'll check out your story about the skates, and if it's true, we'll do everything we can to clear your name. Do you know Heath's last name?"

Jared shook his head.

"That's fine, Jared." I nodded, feeling a pang of sympathy for him. "We would like to know more about him, though. Can you tell us more about Heath?"

Jared opened his mouth, then hesitated, his eyes darting around the room as if he were searching for the right words. Then, slowly, he began to talk.

"Heath... he would use my skates. He used to rent the black ones, always the fancy new black ones. Then, one day he saw me and said 'nice skates.' Then he took *my* skates. He took them every time. No one else ever borrowed *my* skates, they were old and not fancy. 'The black ones are new and fancy,' I told him. 'Use the black ones.' My manager got angry with me and said

'Jared, you work here. These skates are for our customers and if they want the green and teal skates, they get to use them, and not you.' I don't get to skate anymore. I don't get to have my skates." As he spoke, Jared's entire body shook.

"I'm sorry that happened, Jared."

"Those were *my* skates," he continued. "So, that's why I took them. That's why I stole them from the rink. I hid them in my locker at the rink. Then, one day, where were they? My skates were gone. I couldn't find them. Then I couldn't ever skate ever again. Where did I leave those skates? Then the girls, the girls happened, and suddenly the police were at my door, accusing me of things I didn't do. They asked me where the skates were and I told them I didn't know. I told them I must have lost the skates." He wrapped his long, skinny arms around himself and began rocking back and forth in the chair. "I was always losing things. Losing my mind, too."

Clint glanced at me and I could tell from his look that he was listening closely. We were finally getting somewhere. I didn't know if Heath was real or a figment of his imagination, but at least he was giving us new details about the case.

Jared's face contorted in pain. "They said they *knew* I had stolen them. They had video of me leaving the rink with the skates. I told them, 'I stole the skates. And then I couldn't find the skates.' Then it was all over. I was in a cell with time to think. Time to think about how I love skating and how I missed the rink. How the icy air would blast into my face and fill my lungs with the freshest air. Do you know something?"

"What, Jared?" I asked.

"There is no ice air where they sent me. Only piss, vomit, dust, and rust air. I had time to think about Heath stealing my skates when we were at the rink. I had time to think of how he might steal them from me, for keeps, after I stole them from the rink for *my* keeps. Heath had stolen them from me just like that. The police couldn't find the skates. And when I tried to tell them about Heath, it was too late. I was already locked up. They didn't listen. They never listened. They told me I murdered the girls so many times that I believed I must have. But no, I didn't. I didn't kill the little birdies."

The sources I'd had in the Seattle police department had been unwilling to give me anything definitive. Probably because they didn't *have* anything definitive. All they had was speculation. Speculation that other suspects were being ignored. My bet was that Heath was a real person, and he was the suspect they'd ignored once they set their sights on Jared.

Either way, Jared's story left me believing that he had nothing to do with the original murders. He was so distressed. He was so weak looking. There were still so many questions to answer, but at least now, we had a new lead to follow.

Clint stood up slowly, and I knew right away it was a mistake. Jared recoiled slightly, afraid. Clint said, "Are you sure you can't remember a last name for Heath? A sense of where we might find him?"

"Why didn't you find and arrest Heath in the first place?" Jared demanded.

Clint's eyes were hard. "I had nothing to do with that. But I do have one more question for you, Jared." He paused, choosing his words carefully. "Even if we believe you, that there is a 'Heath' out there who's a killer, how the hell did you know to call Macy hours before he came to Buck Lake, hours before he killed Cara?"

Jared blinked, then looked at the ground. "I want a lawyer. I'm done talking."

Clint's frustration was palpable. "We are trying to help you, Jared."

"I said the magic word," Jared spat. "Lawyer."

Clint sighed. "Fine, we'll see if we can track down your lawyer for you," he muttered as he motioned for me to follow him out of the interrogation room.

CHAPTER 25

"JARED'S more ill than I originally thought," I said as we stepped out into the hallway. "I'm starting to believe he didn't kill those girls over in Seattle, but your last question was spot on, Clint." I let out a long breath. "His obsession with those skates… he just seems, innocent somehow. Is that crazy?"

Clint cocked his head, halfway between agreement and skepticism. "His obsession with those skates is bizarre, to be sure. But losing them may have been what made him snap and kill the girls. After all, the bloody laces. And the way he talks about Heath is just... strange. Multiple personalities?"

I nodded. "I have to admit, I had the same thought. But I don't know. I'd like to get a look at this guy's medication list. Could have been off them for days. Maybe weeks even."

Clint scratched his chin. "I would like to see us get a hold of his medications, too. But we can't have access to his medical information unless there's imminent danger."

I frowned. "The way he talks, it sounds like there might be."

Maria and Carlo approached us, having emerged from the conference room. "How's it going in there?" Maria asked, nodding toward the door to the interview room, where Jared now waited for us to return.

Clint filled them in on Jared's strange admissions and his insistence on the existence of Heath.

Carlo was skeptical. "I mean, we sure Heath is a person? Not like the tooth-fairy or something?"

"I believe him," I said. "At least, I think I do."

"Okay," Carlo said, "But I've been through the old files, and the trial records. No mention of a 'Heath.' Macy, when you covered the case, was there any mention of a 'Heath'?"

"No, but—"

"No offense," Carlo continued, "but the guy spent twenty years in a nuthouse. Maybe he made Heath up to cope."

I took some offense to the term "nuthouse," but held my words.

Clint held up both hands. "I need to think about our next moves, and we're not gonna crack this case standing in the hallway." He pointed at Maria. "What about the Bob thing, Nephew Bob?"

Maria shook her head. "There's nothing there. He cooperated fully. Booked his flight right when he heard his uncle had died. We've got receipts, boarding passes. Timing checks out. We called around Des Moines. A few references he gave us. Sounds like he's broke, and a crappy businessman. Two bankruptcies in the last eight years. He was eager as hell to get here, but not to kill his uncle or any girls. Uncle Bob wasn't rich, but the little he had was worth flying in for."

Clint said, "At least that narrows it down a bit."

Next, Clint instructed Maria to contact the lawyer who'd worked on Jared's parole case, hoping to gain some insight into his past and see if he was aware of the Heath angle. To Carlo he assigned the task of getting ahold of Jared's doctor and to get us his medication list, if he'd release it.

Finally, he said, "Macy, I want you to review his medications and find out if any need to be given if he's held overnight. I know you think he's innocent, but I'm not so sure. Either way, I want this thing done as close to the book as possible."

CHAPTER 26

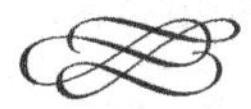

As sunlight filtered through the curtains, I awoke to the familiar sound of crashing waves and the cacophony of seagulls on the beach outside my house. I rubbed the sleep from my eyes and glanced over at Gonzo, who seemed to be waiting for me, his big, expectant eyes focused on my every move.

"We ate all the moussaka last night," I mumbled, still half asleep. "All gone." I held up my empty hands and turned my palms back and forth to prove it.

Gonzo responded with a soft, growling whine-bark, then looked back and forth from me to the bed with wild eyes, alternating standing on his front paws—left, right, left—like he was trying to decide whether to jump on the bed to wake me or scurry off to his own bed for comfort. Seeing that I didn't intend to get up any time soon, he ultimately scuttled back to his little bed.

I tried to ignore Gonzo's occasional soft whine, but then wondered whether he was thinking that I'd suffered the same fate as Bob. "Alright, buddy." I stood and stretched at the side of the bed, looking out at Gonzo, who began doing the same from the safety of his bed. "I believe both you and I are still alive. Let's get outside for a walk and see if we can't take a deep breath of fresh sea air and have it confirm my suspicions of our sentience."

I scooped up Gonzo in his nest, folding the dog bed into the taco shape he and I had agreed was a comfortable position for both of us. Gonzo poked his head in and out of the bed, spun a few times, dug at the material, and then nestled. The straps my mother had sewn on the bed fit perfectly and allowed me to use both hands to carry out my life duties with Gonzo at my side.

We stepped outside, and the cool morning air gently brushed against my face. The beach was a vast expanse of sand broken up by scattered driftwood and rocks spotted with barnacles. The waves lapped rhythmically against the shore, creating a soothing soundtrack that never failed to calm me.

Gonzo's head peeked out from his taco bed, his tiny black ears perked up as he took in the sights and smells around him. I smiled, watching his pink tongue dart out to lick his now salted nose in delight. It was a small victory for both of us—me, getting him outside, and him, enjoying the sensory overload that came with our beach walk.

As much as I wanted to let Gonzo walk the beach on his own, I knew better than to risk being bitten by his tiny, razor-sharp teeth attempting to take him out of the bed myself. There was also the issue of his size. He would have made a nice snack for a bald eagle. I once read in the paper about an eagle's nest that dropped out of a tree in the area and was found to have a dozen or so pet collars stashed in it. With Gonzo's temperament, he might be a fair match for an eagle. Not worth the risk, though.

The thought reminded me that I needed to get him a collar. Bob had neglected to. Or maybe Gonzo had already been taken up by an eagle and lost his collar. I chuckled, imagining the fight, with Gonzo eventually slipping his collar and running back home. I tried to imagine someone putting

Gonzo in a collar. Anyone who tried would likely leave the ordeal with fewer fingers than they'd started with. But it would be a shame if he took off from my arms and no one knew where to send him. I didn't want the little fellow to fall into the wrong talons.

Our walk led me by the Hansville Café, where I stopped to grab a cup of coffee. The owner, a handsome guy around my age, was busy attending to customers. He was a former NYPD detective who'd bought the joint when he moved to the area somewhat recently, the one who'd confirmed seeing Cara and her friends at his store. As I waited for my coffee, I tried to catch his eye with a flirtatious smile, but he seemed preoccupied with the morning rush. In fact, he appeared more interested in meticulously inspecting all the food that came out of the kitchen than anything else. Who did he think he was, Gordon Ramsay?

I sighed inwardly, deciding I'd definitely lost all knowledge of how to flirt.

Coffee in hand, I strolled back to the beach, my thoughts drifting to Jared. He was supposed to be released that morning. His lawyer had shown up late last night, after which Jared had refused to answer any more questions. Though I believed that he wasn't our killer, I also knew that he was still hiding something, or perhaps wasn't able to share something important through the fog of his mental illness.

I plopped down on the sand, crossing my legs and staring out at the Puget Sound. Gonzo tucked himself deep inside the bed to be protected from the worst of the wind.

"You know what would go good with this coffee, Gonzo?" I asked. I didn't wait for a reply. "The blueberry coffee cake Bridget is making for her Saturday brunch." It was times like these that I wished we still lived under the same roof. Although I was the one who harbored the recipe, Bridget was the one who had made it half a dozen times in the last two years. I would likely nurse a spoon of peanut butter for breakfast on my drive to the office today.

The salty breeze whipped my hair around my face and I was just starting to feel at peace with the world when my phone buzzed with an incoming call. It was Kenny. Why was he calling and why was he calling so early in the morning? Reluctantly, I answered.

"Hey, Mac," he said, his voice surprisingly gentle. "I heard about that case you're working on. I think I might have something that could help."

I couldn't believe my ears. "Kenny, how would you know anything about this case? And why are you calling me?"

Kenny sighed. "Look, I've been following it in the news. I talked to Frank, and—"

"Frank?" I cut him off. "The same Frank who crashed his truck into my vegetable garden and took out half of the greenhouse?"

"C'mon, Mac. He's a good guy deep down."

"*Very* deep down, maybe."

"Anyway," Kenny continued, "he told me that around the time of the murder, he was at the bar in town."

"The little café in Hansville?"

"They *do* sell beer, honey."

I was going to shoot back that just because a place sells beer, doesn't mean it's a bar, but instead I said, "Don't call me honey."

"Mac, be serious. He said he heard a car start its engine."

"So what?" I snapped back.

"So… it was around the time of the murder. And, he *knows* the car. It's rare."

I frowned, skeptical. "How can anyone tell the difference between car startup sounds?"

Kenny huffed. "You never cared about my passion for cars, Macy."

I put the phone on mute and rolled my eyes while Kenny

continued to lecture me for my lack of spousal appreciation. "Gonzo, can you believe this guy? He still thinks he can impress me." Gonzo looked up at me with wide, sympathetic eyes.

I unmuted the phone as Kenny continued, his tone condescending. "Ya know, kid, the startup sounds of different vehicles is like a symphony to my ears. Take a nineties Jeep Cherokee, for instance. Those old gas-guzzling engines have a signature rumble when they start up, like a bear waking up from hibernation. The straight-six engine on those Cherokees had a nice, deep growl, like they were ready to tackle any terrain. Pure, unadulterated American muscle."

Gonzo tilted his head, seemingly intrigued by Kenny's car talk. I rolled my eyes again, but kept listening. Slight as it might be, there was a chance Kenny was actually getting somewhere.

"Then you've got your 2010 Prius and your 2020 Porsche—two completely different beasts. The Prius, with its hybrid engine, it's like a ninja, all stealthy and quiet. You barely know it's on, and that's 'cause the electric motor only takes over when its battery gets depleted after you start it up."

I couldn't help but smile at his enthusiasm. "And what about the Porsche, Kenny?"

Kenny had always promised me a Porsche, you know, when our ship came in with the cryptocurrency money.

He laughed. "Ah, the 2020 Porsche, that's a whole different story. You hear that baby fire up, and you know you're dealing with a high-performance machine. It's got a refined purr, like a cat ready to pounce. So, Mac, when you hear these engines, you gotta listen with your heart, not just your ears, 'cause each one tells a different story. That's what I know, and it's what Frank knows, too."

By the end of his monologue, I was bored to tears, but I was glad to have Gonzo to pet behind the ears as Kenny rambled on. Finally, he got to the point. "Frank swears the car that started up right before the murder was a nineties Jeep Cherokee. He's never wrong about this stuff, Mac."

"You sure he can tell that from just listening?"

"Damn right." I could almost see Kenny's cocky smirk through the phone. "4.0-liter inline-6 engine."

As much as I didn't want to admit it, I was grateful for the information. Maybe he could sense my moment of weakness because the next thing he said was, "Mac, if I were to ever come back to Washington and got my act together, think we might give it another shot?"

I paused for half a second, which was half a second too long. Give Kenny half a second and he takes twenty years, all your money, and your nursing license.

"So you're thinking about it?" Kenny asked, his voice full of boyish mirth. "Must've gotten that cashola I sent?"

Truth was, I still had a softness for the guy that went way back. Kenny and I had been highschool sweethearts, but had broken up when I moved to Seattle to go to UW. When I was at my lowest after Bruce disappeared, Kenny and I got back together and he never once blamed or shamed me for what happened. He was just as perplexed as everyone else.

"No, Kenny." Despite the pang of nostalgia, I knew better than to let it sway me. My mom was fond of pointing out that, when Bruce left, at least he left me with five figures in cash. Kenny left me six figures in debt *and* with no way to earn a living. If I ever did marry anyone ever again, all of our possessions would be in my name and my husband would have to wear an ankle bracelet tracking device.

There was a silence on the other end of the line, and I could almost hear him processing my 'No,' like an engine trying to turn over in a car that needed a new transmission.

"Alright, Mac. I understand," he said softly. "Just... take care of yourself, okay?"

"You too, Kenny," I replied before hanging up.

I stood, dusting the sand off my clothes, and took a deep breath.

I looked down at Gonzo, who had been loyally by my side during the entire conversation. The tiniest wingman in history. I scratched behind his little black ears, his white-tipped tail wagging back and forth like a frenetic metronome keeping time with *vivacissimo* speed.

"Gonzo," I said, my voice filled with determination, "Kenny is wrong ninety-nine percent of the time, but on this one, I'm gonna trust him. We need to talk to Clint."

Gonzo barked in agreement. We were learning to speak each other's language.

Despite the emotional turmoil of the day, I couldn't afford to wallow in self-pity.

Saturday or no, I had a job to do.

CHAPTER 27

THE WORLD OUTSIDE IS A BLUR, a harsh kaleidoscope of colors and shapes.

Thoughts, they buzz, swarm in his head, stinging, never quiet.

Meds, the poison, taken or not? They want to poison him, don't they?

His plan failed. The others didn't play their part, didn't fly in formation. He can't understand why they refused, why they resisted. The truth is the truth is the truth.

Finally, the metropolis fades behind him as he reaches his sanctuary, a small cabin nestled in the woods half an hour from Seattle. The city surrenders to the woods' embrace, a haven, where sanity's chokehold loosens. The engine of the Dodge Caravan dies in the driveway in front of his abode.

The cabin, a hodgepodge of scavenged materials and remnants of a life once lived, teeters on the edge of reality. A place where he can escape the suffocating grip of sanity that threatens to choke him. The walls here, covered in scribbles, scratches, and manic drawings, hold the echoes of his twenty-year confinement, a sharp contrast to the sterile walls of the psychiatric prison.

He is finally allowed pointed objects again, and he expresses his feelings using markers and a scalpel blade. Intricate birds have been carved into the drywall, tiny scratches defining each barbule, the feathers scratched in with delicate and accurate detail. The incoherent labels and words and angry slashes complete the picture.

And the birds. Stuffed and staring into the center of the room with beaded eyes. Their individual perches fastened to the walls in no particular pattern, like birds lighting on a tree randomly, each having claimed a branch.

He hasn't taken his medications in over a month. He feels like himself again. He has energy and thoughts of his own. He knows the thoughts are a riddle, but at their core is something very real.

He hears the voice of his lawyer playing over in his mind, whispering assurances before they let him out. The lawyer assures him everything is under control, the police will cease their harassment.

Lies, perhaps.

The lawyer could be with the police. No, that is illegal. And yet. Doubt gnaws, worming through his being. They have locked him up before and won't hesitate to do so again.

Birds flit through the trees outside, their songs a cacophony of overlapping chatter that mirrors his own thoughts.

His plan has failed, crumbled like the delicate wax wings of Icarus flying too close to the sun. Desperation claws at him, tearing away the thin veil of sanity to which he clings. He needs a new plan, something to anchor him to the whirlwind of thoughts that threaten to sweep him away.

Macy.

He can't convince her the easy way, but there is another path, a darker one. The edges of his vision blur, tunneling into a singular focus. If the easy way won't work, then he'll make her see things the hard way.

Whatever it takes to pull her into his world, into the swirling chaos that is his reality. Into the truth of what happened.

The thought lingers, an ominous shadow on the edge of his consciousness. Within him he holds a storm that can burst forth at any moment.

That, only that, will make her see.

He will take what she cares for most.

CHAPTER 28

THE ROAD STRETCHED out before me, an asphalt artery carved through thickly set trees. The rain drizzled lazily on the windshield, smearing the landscape into a blurry impressionist painting. I could feel the weight of the day pressing on my chest, making it harder to breathe. Gonzo would have been a welcome distraction, but he was back home guarding the place from his little bed.

I picked up my phone and dialed Clint. It rang a few times before going to voicemail. "Hey, Clint, it's Macy. I'm headed into the office. Give me a call back when you get a chance."

I was about to turn on the radio when my phone rang, displaying an unfamiliar number. I answered hesitantly. "Hello?"

"Macy, is that you?" slurred a voice on the other end. It took a moment to recognize it as Frank, Kenny's friend. Judging by his voice—not to mention everything I knew about the guy—he was drunk.

"Frank? Why are you calling me?" I asked, gritting my teeth.

"Kenny said you wanted to talk?" he mumbled, the sound of clinking glasses in the background.

I sighed. "Yeah, I guess I did. Look, I heard you were at the café the night of the murder. Did you see or hear anything strange?"

Frank hiccuped, then said, "Yeah, yeah, I did. Just before the time they think the girl was killed, I heard a Jeep Cherokee start up outside. It revved its engine, then took off. Was weird because the place was dead that night. Didn't see anyone get in or out of it. Kinda like it was waiting there."

"Are you sure it was a Cherokee?" I asked, my investigative instincts kicking in.

"Uh, yeah, I'm sure. I used to have one, remember? I know what they sound like," he insisted, his voice slightly more focused.

I nodded, even though he couldn't see me. "Okay, thanks, Frank. I'll keep that in mind."

"Another thing. I saw the girl."

"You what?"

"The girl who was killed. Saw her there with her friends."

"Hold on." I pulled over to the side of the road so I could focus. "You saw Cara, the girl who was killed, at the café the night she was murdered?"

"Yup."

"And you didn't tell anyone yet because…"

He didn't answer.

"Frank?"

"I remembered that engine, but couldn't put two and two together to give the cops that info, you know? I was drunk that night. I was even more drunk the next day when they questioned me. I've been too drunk for too long. But, all that is about to change."

If Frank were about to change, he hadn't started yet. So far, I'd only ever known him to change for the worse.

The line fell silent again.

I was about to hang up when he blurted out, "Hey, Macy, I

heard you're looking to sell the auto repair shop. I'd like to buy it from you."

I nearly choked on my own spit. "Are you serious, Frank? Where would you even get the money for that? You've never had a dime to your name."

"Times have changed, Macy," he slurred, sounding almost proud. "I came into some money."

"Really, Frank?" I scoffed. "You expect me to believe that?"

"Cross my heart, Macy. You know what kind of beer I'm drinking right now? Sierra Nevada Pale Ale. That's the good stuff. My aunt died and left me a quarter million bucks. I'm gonna get sober, then I want to run The Wrench King."

I hesitated, unsure of what to make of any of this. "Well, I'll think about it, Frank. Right now I gotta talk to my boss at the WSP."

After we hung up, I called Clint and told him about my conversation, promising to get into the office as soon as possible. I ended the call as I merged onto the highway, leaving Poulsbo and heading toward Bremerton. Tall trees lined the road, their branches dripping with rainwater, and the dark, heavy clouds and gray skies seemed to mirror my mood.

My mind wandered back to the years I'd spent with Kenny, the memories a bittersweet mixture of good times and bad. I remembered the way he'd laugh at his own jokes, that infectious, lighthearted chuckle that had drawn me to him in the first place. But then I thought about the arguments, the shouting matches that seemed to escalate with every passing year. And the theft. I couldn't forgive him for putting my career as a nurse in jeopardy.

Yet, as much as I'd judged him over the years, I knew I'd played a role in it too. Maybe I'd been wrong to give up my job as a crime reporter to move out to Hansville all those years ago. I'd told myself it would only be for a couple years, then we'd move back to Seattle. Maybe I'd even go back to work as a journalist, maybe stick with the nursing stuff if I grew to like the field. Such things to be. We'd been so young, so full of hope and dreams that had slowly crumbled away.

But through it all, we'd been blessed with our daughter, Bridget. She was the light of my life, the one thing that made it all worth it. The thought of her brought a bittersweet smile to my face as tears threatened to spill.

I blinked them away, driving through the rain-slicked streets, the distant lights of Bremerton twinkling like stars through the mist. I never thought I'd be 45 years old, owning an auto repair shop and working with the police. Life had a funny way of taking you places you never expected.

A few stray tears escaped, rolling down my cheeks as I took a deep breath.

Feeling emotional, I decided to call Bridget. I knew she was probably still asleep, but I just needed to hear her voice. When it went to voicemail, I took a deep breath and began to speak.

"Hey, Bridge. I know you're probably still asleep now, but I just wanted to tell you how much I love you. Give me a call later and tell me how the coffee cake turned out, and how the brunch went. You're the best thing that's ever happened to me, kiddo. And I wanted to apologize for anything bad I might have said about your dad in the past. We're all imperfect, just trying to do our best on this wet rock we call Earth." I hesitated, then added with a small laugh, "Oh, and I almost forgot to tell you, I got a new little dog named Gonzo. He's a neurotic chihuahua, and he's driving me nuts, but I love him, too. You might think I'm crazy, and you're not wrong." I sighed, feeling a weight lift off my chest. "Anyway, just wanted to let you know I'm thinking of you. Call me when you can. Love you."

As I ended the call, the car seemed to fill with a silence that was comforting and a little lonely. Life was strange and unpredictable, but for the first time in a while, I felt some ray of hope. Maybe it was Gonzo, or maybe it was the realization that, despite everything, I still had people in my life who mattered, like Bridget.

I glanced at the rain-soaked landscape passing by, the trees standing tall and resilient despite having gone through storm after storm. At that moment, I felt strong too. No matter what life threw at me next, I would face the challenge head-on, with determination.

That's what we do, right? Debt, betrayal, dead neighbor Bobs, neurotic chihuahuas, even murders. We keep moving forward, learning and growing, one step at a time, finding strength in the love and connections that bind us all together.

CHAPTER 29

As I pulled into the parking lot of the Washington State Patrol office, my brain was still doing too much work. I wondered, is this really my life now? Do I work for the Washington State Patrol? I was having a touch of imposter syndrome, so I took a deep breath as I stepped out of the car, trying to remind myself that I was here for a reason.

The cool drizzle on my face helped me recognize myself again as I made my way across the parking lot and inside.

In the conference room, I found Carlo, Maria, and Clint gathered around the table. There was a new girl there, too, who couldn't have been more than nineteen years old. She had a wolf haircut with streaks of pink, purple, and green, and a pair of black combat boots that looked like they'd seen their fair share of adventures.

Carlo introduced her as "Katya, or Tech-Girl-K."

Katya pretended to be offended, then said with a grin, "It's Tech-Lady-K." She was short, with tattoos running up and down her arms—a vibrant mosaic of dragons, stars, and intricate patterns. Her eyes sparkled with mischief and intelligence, and she wore a huge smile that was somehow both charming and disarming—the kind of smile that says, *I might be flirting with you, but I might also be hacking your phone to steal your identity.*

I liked her right away.

"Katya runs LEAI," Clint said. "Law Enforcement Artificial Intelligence. Chief gave us the budget to use her and her team on this case as a one time thing.

"We're not cheap," Katya said, "but we're the best. And I don't say that to brag."

Clint smiled as though presenting his own daughter for approval. "Katya dropped out of the University of Washington when she was *sixteen*, when she was a year away from an honors degree in computer science. Tell 'em what you do, Katya."

"Basically, LEAI uses artificial intelligence to combine all available footage with maps and other data to try to figure out which cars *could have* been where and when. I mean, that's what we did in this case. We offer other services as well."

In the center of the room, Katya had set up a large TV, which was connected to a laptop. As we settled into our seats, she began playing a series of videos, explaining that they were the surveillance footage from every single camera in and around Hansville on the night of the murder. Gas stations, driveways, even front porch security cameras that happened to point toward the street.

Her enthusiasm and knowledge were infectious, drawing us all into her world of cutting-edge technology. I found myself confused at times, struggling to keep up with the barrage of information, but Katya was an excellent teacher. She broke down complex concepts into easily digestible pieces, using analogies and humor to help us understand. The sheer volume of data she'd managed to compile and analyze was astounding.

Her fingers flew across her laptop's keyboard as she pulled up different angles and locations. "Alright," Katya said, her eyes twinkling with excitement, "Those clips were an overview, but

I've managed to narrow it down to twenty-two possible cars that the killer could have driven."

Carlo raised his eyebrows, clearly intrigued. "Impressive. But none of them are the minivan owned by Jared, right?"

Maria leaned in, her expression thoughtful. "I still can't believe they let that guy drive, considering his mental state."

"None are mini-vans," Katya said, "though of course he could have rented or borrowed something else."

I glanced around the room before speaking up, my voice tinged with hope. "Is there any chance one of those cars is a late nineties Jeep Cherokee?"

Katya stared at me for a moment, curiosity flickering in her eyes. Then, without a word, she scrolled forward on the video. We all watched the big screen, the tension in the room mounting as the footage played. "Here," she said, slowing the video down. "Take a look at this."

A dark green Jeep Cherokee appeared on the screen, pulling into a gas station. Katya explained that the location was in Kingston, not even ten miles from the crime scene.

As we watched the man in the hooded sweatshirt exit the vehicle and begin pumping gas, Maria leaned over to me. "Macy, why did you ask about the Jeep Cherokee?"

"Oh..." I hesitated... "something I heard from a very unreliable source." I thought of Frank's slurred voice and claims of coming into a fortune. "Family friend, sort of, said he heard a Jeep Cherokee in the area that night."

"I looked up the interview we did with him after you called," Clint said. "Didn't say anything about it then."

"Right. That's on brand for him, though. He's an unreliable drunk. Unreliable about everything except cars."

The room fell silent as we continued to watch the footage at the gas station. As he pumped the gas, the man's face remained hidden beneath his hood. I didn't recognize him, but there was something about the way he moved that made my skin crawl.

Carlo shifted in his seat, his expression grim. "We need to find out who this guy is."

"Alright," Katya said, breaking the silence. "There's something else. Four minutes after leaving the gas station, that same car was caught on a porch camera driving toward Hansville from Kingston."

I leaned forward, unable to contain my excitement. "That's too close to be a coincidence."

Clint's voice was urgent as he asked, "Can you get a plate number, Katya?"

She nodded, her fingers flying across her keyboard. The image on the screen zoomed in on the Jeep's license plate, the numbers coming into focus.

As Katya worked her magic, Carlo pulled out his own laptop and began typing. "Jared was talking about some guy named Heath, right?" he said, his brow furrowed in concentration.

Clint chimed in. "Sure did, Heath this and Heath that. Fifty-fifty he was either lying, or delusional, but..."

As Carlo typed, I exchanged glances with Maria, feeling a mix of excitement and dread.

Carlo's fingers danced across his keyboard as he entered the plate number, waiting for the system to return a result.

The seconds felt like hours as we all held our breath.

Finally, Carlo looked up, his face plastered with a cocky grin. "We got our guy, I think. The Jeep is registered to a man named Heath Spencer."

CHAPTER 30

His Bremerton stomping grounds sprawl before him and he knows this world like he knows his teal and green ice skates. Olympic. The college he would have gone to, but they didn't have any skating classes.

He stands in front of the apartment building, which shelters the innocent from his twisted intentions.

Twisted, he thinks, but in a good way. A true way.

With each breath, his hatred for the city consumes him. His only solace there had been the ice rink and the little Rota Vista park, where he spent hours after school during the winters watching the Peregrine Falcons hunt and the Pelagic Cormorants nesting underneath the Warren Avenue Bridge.

Bremerton, a bedroom city of Seattle, was also a bedroom city to the naval base. Navy men and women haunt the corners of his vision, their presence a phantom pain, a cruel reminder of his father's torment.

Strange how in his more coherent moments—like this one—all the memories come back, clean and bright. And terrible.

He skulks outside the apartment, his gaze locked on the

entrance, feverish and unyielding. The photo trembles in his hand, revealing a girl with the face of her mother.

She is the target, the source of his dark fixation.

He will move in like a falcon. He will make a spectacular drop from high above. The minute he sees her, his high-speed dive will take her by surprise and he will have her.

He is like the falcon after all. The male Duck Hawk is compact, usually smaller than the opposite sex. But, despite his diminutive size, he will swoop down and take the girl with the force of a bird-eating raptor.

A voice slices through the air, making his heart skip a beat. "Bridget!"

He whips his head toward the sound, finding a grassy patch where two friends embrace. Their laughter grates on his nerves as if the universe were mocking him. He feels the feathers on his back rise.

The friends speak for a moment, then one walks away, leaving the girl behind.

"That's her," he twitters, his voice undulating like an American Robin. His thoughts dance and chitter, a blend of frenetic darkness and depravity.

The girl is a reflection of her mother, the mother he thought was on his side. The thought of that tricky-tricky cuckoo mother of hers fuels his anger. He steps toward the baby bird.

A pigeon lands on the picnic table nearby, trying to distract him. He needs to focus.

His internal voice surfaces, sounding like a Blue Jay: "Focus, focus." His attention snaps back to the girl, the darkness within him eager to be unleashed.

It is time.

She holds a cake in one hand, her phone to her ear with the other, but she isn't chirping back, her attention likely absorbed by a message, her guard down, vulnerable. He chooses a wide arc, ensuring she remains blissfully unaware of the rapidly encroaching darkness.

His eyes dart to his car, a mere twenty feet away, an escape vessel waiting in the wings. His pulse quickens, the anticipation a symphony of dread and delight.

As he nears, the girl switches from listening to speaking, leaving a message of her own. Her words hang in the air, a fragile thread of connection. "Thanks for your message, Mom. I'm headed to brunch. There's a guy I'm thinking of asking out who's supposed to be there. I hope he likes blueberry coffee cake. Thanks again for the recipe, it turned out great. Love you, too."

Now a twisted specter, closing in at her back, he presses a toy gun into her side. The burrowing owl hisses like a rattlesnake to scare off squirrels. This plastic gun will do. Humans are no smarter than squirrels.

"Don't turn around," he warns. "Close your eyes. I'm going to take your wing. You're coming with me, birdie."

She drops her phone. She drops her cake. Turns a little, then stops. Her face shakes in terror.

Time slows, the world around them is static.

The pigeon hops down to peck at the cake crumbs. The girl is rushed into the van. The crumbs and the girl will vanish.

The dance of predator and prey has begun.

CHAPTER 31

"Gotta give it to you, Macy." Clint changed lanes, swerving around a semi-truck. "I wasn't sure Heath was real."

"Thanks," I said, looking out at the overcast sky, which gave the landscape a moody atmosphere, making the industrial zones, imposing bridges, and lush greenery blur together in a mesmerizing swirl of grays. "I know our hunches lie sometimes, so I'm glad mine got a win on this one. But it's not only that," I continued. "He was stalking me on the ferry." I'd pulled up a photo of Heath from the website of his accounting firm and, just like that, I was staring into the face of the man who'd been following me. The mysterious man with dyed blond hair and a spray tan who'd stalked me on the ferry had been this man, Heath.

"So somehow he knew we were on the case and… what?"

"Doesn't make sense to me, either," I said. "Let's focus on bringing him in. We can figure out the whys later."

I checked the rearview mirror, where Carlo and Maria tailed us like a loyal sidekick. We were halfway to Tacoma, having found multiple addresses for Heath. The plan was for them to check Heath's office about ten minutes past Tacoma, while Clint and I headed to his luxury apartment.

The miles ticked by, and I checked my phone, finding a voicemail from Bridget. I grinned as I listened to her message, her voice a welcome distraction. Sometimes a quick call from her was enough to brighten my day.

Feeling a surge of gratitude, I counted what was left of the cash Kenny had sent before texting Bridget: "Hey Bridge, just heard your message. You're the best. Let's grab pizza at Alfredo's tonight or in the next day or two. And believe it or not, dinner's on your dad." I hesitated before sending a follow-up message. "Okay, I know I said I'd avoid the passive-aggressive stuff. But seriously, your dad came through with some cash. Love you, Bridge."

As I hit send, a memory resurfaced. I recalled the sound of broken porcelain and the sight of Bridget's piggy bank shards peeking through a thin garbage bag one morning as I took out the trash. I remember thinking at the time, *what kind of man steals his eight-year-old daughter's piggy bank?*

And that's exactly what I'd screamed at him when Bridget left for school that morning. Long story short, he'd sobered up for a while after that. I secretly bought her a new piggy bank and put some change in it, shielding her from her father's transgression. After that, we'd had more good years together. Kenny got some help and we pulled ourselves out of debt. But the stress of owning The Wrench King had proven to be more than he could handle. Secretly, he began to break our bank again.

"Let's re-examine the Heath file."

Clint's voice shook me out of my daydream and I opened the information Katya had sent about Heath. The file read like a formal summary, gleaned from public records, and I read it aloud.

"Heath Spencer, age 47. Two vehicles registered in his name:

a 1998 Jeep Cherokee and a 2021 Porsche. Owns a condo in Tacoma. Born and raised in Seattle. Graduated from the University of Washington with a degree in accounting. Currently a tax accountant, running his own successful firm, Spencer and Co. Married in 2004 to Vanessa Spencer, formerly Vanessa Jokic, a high school teacher. They have one daughter, Amanda, born in 2006. Enjoys sailing and is a member of the Tacoma Yacht Club. No criminal history. Heath's daughter is around the same age as Cara." The thought chilled me.

Clint glanced my way, asking, "Is there anything in there that connects him to our case, other than the Jeep?"

I sifted through the files, mostly irrelevant stuff like his business license, property deeds, and evidence of his yacht club membership. "Nothing obvious," I admitted, feeling a twinge of frustration. "But there has to be something we're missing."

My eyes widened as I stumbled on a crucial detail: Heath volunteered as a coach for a local youth hockey team, sponsored by his accounting firm. The team was called The Spencer and Co. Raiders.

"Clint, get a load of this," I said, excitement rising in my voice. "Heath coaches a youth hockey team."

Clint's eyebrows shot up. "That's something, all right. Hockey, skates, wax laces. Hate to admit it, but it fits Jared's ramblings."

As we neared Tacoma, I asked Clint, "What's our move when we get there?"

"First we have to see if he's home," Clint explained. "If he is, and he's dumb enough to chat with us, we poke around his place, see if there's anything that ties him to the crime scene or the victims. And if we stumble onto something concrete, we'll haul him in."

"And if he's not home? Can we bust down the door or, like..." I trailed off, knowing how naive I sounded.

"Well, unfortunately, the Fourth Amendment would take issue with that."

I nodded, the gravity of the situation sinking in. If Heath was indeed the killer, we were about to confront a man who had brutally murdered at least one girl, possibly more.

CHAPTER 32

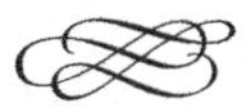

THE MOMENT we stepped into the lobby of Heath's fancy apartment building in Tacoma, I knew we were a long way from Hansville.

The high ceilings were adorned with delicate chandeliers, casting a warm, opulent glow over the polished marble floors. The walls boasted intricate molding and gold-leaf accents, giving the space a regal air. In the corner, a grand piano stood quietly, waiting for someone to awaken its keys.

I felt out of place in these ritzy surroundings, like a pauper in a palace. But I tried to keep my cool, remembering that I was here on important business. Clint, on the other hand, was busy craning his neck to get a better look at the tall, muscular man walking through the lobby.

"Is that… what's his name?" he whispered excitedly. "The Seahawk's starting running back? Davis, or Davies?"

"I don't know, Clint." I shrugged, my eyes taking in the attentive doormen and the sophisticated security system. "I've got a feeling we're not in Kansas anymore."

We approached the front desk, where an older man greeted us with a formal nod. He had a dignified air about him, like someone who took great pride in protecting the building and its residents. Clint flashed his badge and explained our situation.

The man's eyes narrowed as he listened, then he picked up the phone to call Heath's apartment. There was no answer. Clint insisted that we needed to go upstairs to knock on the door, but the doorman was reluctant to let us up.

"I can't just let you go up there without Mr. Spencer's permission," he said, his tone firm.

"Listen," Clint argued, "we have reason to believe Mr. Spencer might be connected to an ongoing murder investigation. It's important that we check his apartment as soon as possible."

The doorman hesitated, glancing between Clint and me as he weighed his options. Finally, he agreed to take us up in the elevator, but on the condition that he accompany us.

As we waited for the elevator doors to open, I felt a knot forming in my stomach. If we got in, what would we find in his apartment? I imagined finding Jared's ice skates, one of the wax laces missing.

On the ride up to the eighteenth floor, Clint asked the doorman a few questions, trying to nail down anything he could about Heath's life and his routines. Each time, the man answered with a curt, "I really can't say, officer."

My nerves were on edge and I found myself drumming my fingers against my thigh, an old habit I hadn't fully committed to trying to shake. Clint, on the other hand, appeared calm and collected, his eyes fixed on the ascending dial above the elevator doors. Finally, the elevator came to a smooth stop and the doors slid open to reveal a plush, carpeted hallway. The doorman led us down the corridor, his steps measured and deliberate. He stopped in front of a polished wooden door, adorned with a gleaming brass number.

This was it, Heath Spencer's apartment.

With a deep breath, I steeled myself for whatever lay on the other side. The moment of truth.

We lifted the brass knocker and let it fall, our ears close to the door as though we might be able to hear Heath stashing evidence through the solid, three-inch-thick, sound deadening entrance.

Clint knew that the doorman was not about to let us in Heath's room without a warrant or consent from Heath himself so, after three-minutes, we gave up and headed back to the lobby. We'd gotten nowhere. The Fourth Amendment had us up the creek without a paddle.

Clint had a mischievous glint in his eyes, clearly plotting something. "Watch this," he said.

Clint approached a well-dressed woman as she exited the elevator, "Excuse me, ma'am. Do you know a Heath Spencer? What's he like? Has he been acting strangely lately?"

The woman looked taken aback, mumbling something incoherent before hurrying away.

Clint repeated the act with the next few residents who walked through the lobby, asking them loud, intrusive questions about Heath. It seemed he was intent on making a scene.

Anything for justice.

I could tell that Clint's antics were starting to annoy the doorman, who was watching us with a mix of irritation and concern. After Clint had scared away an elderly couple, the doorman approached us, his face stern. "If you promise to stop harassing my residents, I will answer your questions," he said firmly. "Any that I can."

We walked back to the front desk, where Clint began grilling the doorman about Heath. "What's his schedule like? Was he home last week or traveling? When was the last time you saw him driving his nineties Cherokee?"

The doorman's answers were vague, and I could tell he was trying to be protective of Heath's privacy. It was clear we would have to push harder if we wanted to get the information we needed.

Clint leaned in, his voice low and threatening. "Look, we need to know if Heath was at home between six and ten last Tuesday night. This is important. We need someone to cooperate with us. Is it going to be you or the residents I interrupt on their way to their lavish apartments? Do you think the residents here would be concerned to find out that they may be living next door to a serial killer?"

The doorman hesitated, glancing between us as if weighing his options. "Okay, okay." He reluctantly agreed to help us. "I'll see what I can find out."

He turned to his computer terminal, his fingers tapping away on the keyboard. "You said last Tuesday night, right? I can get you exit and entry records, but promise me you won't let this come back on me. I'm a relic around here. They might think they can run this place without me, but I'd like to see them try."

Clint stared at him, his expression hard and unyielding.

The doorman sighed, resigning himself to his fate. "According to our records," he began, his voice a loud whisper, "Heath's Cherokee left our underground garage at four in the afternoon, and he didn't return until the next morning around nine."

My heart raced as I processed this new piece of information. It fit the timeline of the murders perfectly. This was another massive breakthrough. I looked over at Clint, who was clearly thinking the same thing.

"Thank you for your help," I said to the doorman, trying to sound sincere and professional through my excitement.

"Appreciate it," Clint said, pulling me away from the desk to talk in private. "He might have driven, but if he took the ferry we might be able to get some footage Katya didn't yet have."

"But, why nine in the morning?" I wondered aloud. "Wouldn't he have taken an earlier boat? If he killed Cara around 8:30, he could have taken a ferry around nine or ten, or just driven home and been back in time for the late night shows."

Clint's phone rang and he answered quickly, his voice tense as he listened to the person on the other end. I could only hear his side of the conversation—an occasional "Okay" or "Hmm"—but Clint's physical responses had me on the edge of my seat. I felt like I was waiting in line at Disneyland, the anticipation building as I got closer to the ride.

"Yeah, okay... Where?" Clint asked, his brow furrowed in concentration.

I shifted my weight from one foot to the other, trying to be patient, but failing miserably.

Clint nodded. "I'll call you from the car."

He turned to me, his eyes filled with urgency. "Let's go!" he exclaimed, already speed-walking through the lobby.

"Go where?" I called, hurrying to keep up, my heart pounding, my breath quick with the exertion and excitement.

Clint didn't reply, just raced for the car like the nurse wielding the crash cart to a Code Blue.

I followed him into the car, slamming the door and asking, "Clint, where are we going? Who was that?"

"Carlo." He started the car and peeled out of the parking lot, heading for the freeway. "He and Maria were waiting in front of Heath's business. They spotted him and he fled in his Porsche. They're trying to intercept him now."

CHAPTER 33

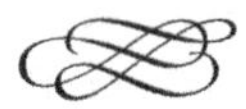

CLINT DIALED Carlo and Maria while easing through a red light.

Maria's voice came through, tense and focused. "We're heading north on I-5, just past the Tacoma Dome. He's driving like a maniac, but we're keeping up."

My stomach lurched as Clint took the I-5 onramp at breakneck speed, then swerved between cars with a precision that was both impressive and terrifying. I gripped the door handle tightly, trying to steady myself as we drove to catch up with Carlo and Maria, who were tailing Heath. The sun glared in my eyes, making it difficult to see clearly as we navigated the moderate Saturday traffic heading towards Seattle.

Clint threaded the needle between cars, trucks, and concrete barriers, my bicep flexing with every jolt to the right, my shoulder flexing with every leftward weave as I tried not to slam my head into Clint or the car window. This ride was either going to improve my neck flexibility or throw off my alignment. In either case, I'd be scheduling a massage therapy appointment as soon as possible.

As we sped along, I caught a glimpse of the iconic Tacoma Dome fading into the distance in the rearview mirror. "Clint, are you sure we should be driving like this?" I asked, my voice shaky as he expertly swerved between lanes, narrowly avoiding a collision with a truck merging onto the highway.

"Don't worry, I'm a pro," he replied, his eyes locked on the road ahead. "Just keep an eye out for Maria's SUV."

My heart pounded as I scanned the expanse of cars, searching for our teammates. Finally, I spotted the familiar vehicle ahead of us. "There they are!" I shouted, pointing at the SUV weaving through traffic.

"Got it," Clint replied, pressing down on the accelerator as we closed the distance between us and Maria and Carlo.

Carlo's voice came through the speaker again. "He's not slowing down, and he's getting more reckless."

The urgency in his voice heightened my own sense of panic. This was no longer just about catching a killer; innocent lives were at stake, including our own. Traffic was moderate, but at speeds like this, he could do a lot of damage.

I blurted out the obvious. "We need to stop him before someone gets hurt."

Heath Spencer's black Porsche appeared up ahead, a sleek predator slicing through traffic. Carlo and Maria's SUV was hot on his tail, weaving in and out of lanes to keep up. My heart was pounding in my chest.

One way or another, we were getting closer to a resolution. I just hoped it wouldn't end in an accident with somebody severely injured. Or dead. Not unlike hour ten on a twelve hour shift, I could smell my own sweat.

Clint's face was tight with tension as he focused on keeping pace. His eyes flicked from side to side, constantly scanning for potential obstacles. Suddenly, a wall of brake lights appeared in front of us, and my breath caught in my throat. A traffic jam had materialized out of nowhere, a snarl of cars and trucks grinding to a near halt on the freeway.

Clint's eyes widened and he slammed on the brakes with a

curse as he threw his right arm in front of me like I was a child and he didn't trust the seat belt to protect me from injury.

But the seatbelt held fast and I felt it forcefully holding my waist in place, punching into my chest, and sawing against my neck.

The tires screeched in protest as we hurtled toward the minivan. Its back window was stickered with five stick figures, indicating the size of the family we were about to smash into. Time seemed to slow down, each second stretching into an eternity as the gap between our car and the minivan closed. I braced myself for impact, my hands gripping the dashboard so tightly my fingers ached.

Miraculously, we stopped just inches from the minivan's bumper. My heart was pumping so hard I was sure it would burst from my chest. I gasped for air as I tried to calm my racing thoughts. Clint looked over at me, his own breathing ragged, and gave me a shaky nod to assure me we were okay.

"Sorry, Mac," he managed to say, still reeling from the near miss.

"Where are they?" I had moved on from the jarring halt and returned my focus to the chase.

In the chaos of the sudden traffic jam, we'd lost sight of Heath's Porsche. I scanned the sea of cars, searching for any sign of him or Carlo and Maria. Desperation clawed at my insides as I realized we might have lost our only chance to catch Heath.

Then, out of the corner of my eye, I saw it. The sleek black Porsche veered off an exit onto a frontage road, disappearing from view as it sped around a curve.

My heart sank, and I looked over at Clint, pointing, my eyes wide with panic. "He exited," I said. He was too far away to catch. "Clint, I think we've lost him."

Clint's face was a mixture of frustration and determination, his jaw set in a grim line. Cars were all around us, boxing us in.

"Not yet," he replied, his voice steely. "We're not giving up that easily."

CHAPTER 34

LIGHTS AND SIREN BLARING, Clint's hands danced on the wheel, expertly backing up, inching forward, and slowly maneuvering the car through the stop-and-go traffic as we tried to regain ground on Carlo, Maria, and Heath. Cars moved to the sides to let us through, but we still weren't able to get up to more than five miles per hour.

Finally, Clint swerved around a car and through a traffic light, where he was able to pick up speed as we saw the tail of Carlo's SUV hugging a curve ahead of us.

Tension coiled in my gut and my fingers ached from gripping the door handle. The rest of my body grew numb. I'd treated enough people for seat belt syndrome during my time in the ER to know that in a day or two I would be needing muscle relaxers to remain at baseline activity.

From frontage road to side street, side streets to the outskirts of SoDo in Seattle, Clint followed Carlo who, we hoped, had Heath in his view.

A flash of black caught my eye and I spotted Heath's Porsche turning down a wide alley. "There!" I shouted, pointing.

Clint instantly swerved to follow.

We were trailing closely behind Carlo and Maria now, the alley's brick walls looming around us. Heath's Porsche suddenly hit a dead end. A massive dumpster had been inexplicably left at the end of the alley, blocking his exit. Frantically, he tried to turn his car around in the tight space. "What the hell is he doing?" I asked.

Clint slowed. "No idea."

There was only four or five feet of space on each side of Carlo's SUV. Not enough room for Heath to pass.

Carlo wasted no time. Before I had time to think, he leapt from his vehicle, gun drawn and ready.

Clint pulled to a stop a dozen yards back. "Wait here," he ordered, leaping out of the car.

My heart pounded in my chest as I watched, breath held. Carlo advanced toward the Porsche, which was still trying to turn around. Back four inches, forward four inches. I had no idea what he was thinking.

Carlo shouted commands for Heath to surrender.

Then, in a split second, everything changed.

Heath finally got the Porsche turned around, then gunned the gas. Tires screeching, the car barreled toward Carlo. I reached for the door handle.

Oh, no.

Carlo stood frozen in shock, and my horror matched his as I realized he might not get out of the way in time. *Pop.*

He fired one round, hitting the windshield but missing Heath.

Clint was shouting something inaudible from behind Carlo's SUV. Maria hopped out, taking cover behind her open door.

"Carlo!" I screamed, but the sound was swallowed by the roar of the engine and the chaos unfolding before my eyes.

The sound of the impact was sickening as the Porsche collided with Carlo's body, sending him careening through the air like a discarded toy. My stomach twisted into knots at the gruesome sight.

Heath's Porsche wasted no time, accelerating with a roar toward Clint, who dove behind the SUV. Grazing the sides of Carlo's SUV with a sickening screech, Heath made it past, then accelerated as he aimed at the even tighter spot between my door and the wall of the alley. There was no way he'd make it.

Picking up speed, the Porsche smashed the sideview mirror only inches from where I sat in the passenger seat. The metal of the door bent and the Porsche slowed, but didn't stop.

As he hit the gas, Heath looked over and flashed a wicked smile.

I crawled over the center console and leapt out Clint's side, dust and debris clouding the air, a hazy veil masking my view as I bolted towards Carlo's crumpled form.

Maria stumbled toward him, too, her face ashen and eyes wide. The unfolding chaos seemed to distort our surroundings, narrowing our focus to the man who lay injured on the ground.

A potent mix of anger and helplessness surged within me, as bitter as the metallic tang of blood in my mouth. I watched Carlo's chest heave with labored breaths.

As we knelt beside Carlo, I took in every detail: the jagged edges of his torn clothes, the beads of sweat glistening on his furrowed brow, and the blood staining the ground beneath him.

CHAPTER 35

"CLINT, CALL 911!" I shouted, my nursing instincts kicking in as I leaned over Carlo's still body.

His consciousness was fading and blood poured from a deep gash on his leg. His breathing was shallow and I knew I was watching life slipping away before my eyes.

Maria knelt by his side, holding his mangled leg and looking around frantically for something to stop the bleeding.

"Maria," I said, my voice shaking. "Help me find something to use as a tourniquet."

Her eyes wide, Maria looked at me with a distant stare, her hands trembling.

I pressed my hands into his upper leg to keep the bloodloss down.

"Yes, he's still breathing," Clint barked at the 911 operator, racing back from the SUV with a medical kit. "We're trying to stop the bleeding now."

"Maria!" I shouted. Her eyes had a strange, glazed-over look, like she might have dissociated. "Maria!"

Maria shook herself into the present and grabbed the emergency kit from Clint, then pulled out a tourniquet that looked only long enough to wrap around a small child's limb. She threw it aside and pulled out a giant roll of duct tape. "Will this work?" she asked, spinning the tape to find the loose end.

"Good thinking," I said. "I think so."

Maria found the end of the tape and handed it to me. Carlo let out a deep groan of pain as I wrapped his leg. "Quick, Clint, you got a lug wrench in there?" I shouted.

He collected the cross-shaped metal tool and handed it to Maria, who was next to me, kneeling beside Carlo.

"Maria, hold that there against his leg."

Maria looked puzzled, but she held the wrench against his leg. "What are we doing?"

I took two passes of the duct tape around his leg and over the center of the lug wrench, then turned the wrench clockwise. The twisting pulled taut the duct tape tightening the makeshift tourniquet, finally getting the bleeding under control.

"I wouldn't have thought to do that in a million years," Clint remarked.

"Carlo, please," Maria pleaded, her voice cracking. "You have to survive this."

"How far out is an ambulance?" I called out to Clint.

"They're telling me ten minutes," Clint said.

"And how far is the hospital?" I asked.

"About ten minutes," Maria said.

"We have to get him in the car and get him to the hospital ourselves if he's gonna make it," I determined.

The three of us hoisted Carlo into the back of Clint's car, adrenaline fueling our strength. Clint gunned the engine, and we tore through the city streets, leaving Carlo's SUV behind.

As I continued to hold the tire iron in place, Maria held his hand, her voice soothing and strong. "Carlo, you're not alone. We're here, and we're not giving up on you."

Clint's knuckles turned white as he gripped the steering

wheel, weaving through traffic as adeptly as any ambulance might. "Hang in there, Carlo. We'll get you to the hospital."

The metallic scent of blood filled the car. In the back seat, Maria held Carlo's upper half over her lap. His legs were draped over mine as I used one hand to vice grip the lug wrench, the other assessing his pulse, which was mildly tachycardic, but his color was not too bad. Maria wiped the sweat from his brow.

Slowly, Carlo opened his eyes.

Through clenched teeth and labored breaths, he locked eyes with me and whispered, "I... love Ma-, Ma-, Mari-..." He shifted his gaze to Maria.

Maria's eyes glistened with tears as she looked deep into his. At that moment, Carlo mustered the strength to utter the final words of his sentence: "Maria's friend." Then he cracked a wide, mocking grin at Maria.

Maria half laughed and half cried, then said, "If you don't die from this, Carlo, I'll either kill you or kiss you." She looked up at me. "Maybe both."

I laughed. "He's still with us."

"Yes, he is," Maria laughed through tears.

"Unfortunately for you," I said, "I think he's gonna make it."

Carlo let out a laugh that turned into a moan.

Clint sped toward the hospital as I focused on keeping Carlo's leg still. Carlo grimaced and moaned with every bump and swerve. I was grateful for his signs of life, but wished that he didn't have to be in pain to express them.

"Keep him talking, Maria," I said, "we want to keep him awake if we can."

Maria kept Carlo in a state of banter between his expressions of pain. The two were in their own little world whispering to each other.

I couldn't hear what they were saying, but I imagined Carlo saying, "You could use a good kiss," and Maria responding, "I'd just as soon kiss a Wookie." In the back of the SUV, sparks were flying within the Rebel Alliance. I kept tight the tourniquet, trying not to eavesdrop on their untimely love connection.

My mind shifted and I struggled to piece together the puzzle. Had Heath been the Waxlace Strangler all along, perhaps driven by some twisted desire to finish what he'd started all those years ago now that Jared had been released? And if so, how had Jared known about his plans in advance? These nagging questions gnawed at the edge of my consciousness.

As we arrived at the hospital, the emergency staff swarmed around us, taking over Carlo's care. I watched as they whisked him away, my heart pounding with fear and hope.

I'd done everything I could.

Now it was up to the medical professionals to save the leg of the man who loved Maria's friend.

CHAPTER 36

THAT NIGHT I returned home to find that my once cozy beachfront house had devolved into a disaster. "What kind of chaotic mess of a person lives here?" I asked Gonzo on my way past the doom piles that littered the dining table. I could barely make out the dark, moonlit beach through the streaks on my dirty window panes. The overflowing baskets of dirty laundry betrayed the fact that I'd been wearing the same outfit for three days. The dirty dishes piled up in the sink were a monument to my culinary failures.

Pacing back and forth in the dimly lit living room, I sipped the cold coffee that I'd discovered in the microwave. It could've been from this morning or two days ago; time was a blur. The chaos of the last few days, weeks, months had thrown off my every routine. But there was one thing I could count on: there was almost always a cold cup of coffee waiting for me in the microwave, and I took comfort in that small, consistent detail.

I'd been at the hospital for five hours. The good news was that Carlo was in stable condition, though his leg still hung in the balance. The bad news was that I hadn't heard back from Bridget and was starting to freak out.

Maybe it was because of the day I'd had, maybe I just needed to hear her voice, but I couldn't shake the feeling that something was wrong. I'd expected a text back about pizza dinner, and had checked my phone every few minutes while at the hospital. I dialed her number; straight to voicemail.

Next I began calling her friends, hoping one of them might know where she was. Molly and Samantha didn't answer. No one in my daughter's generation answers their phone. Bryce—a wanna-be mechanic she'd dated for two weeks before realizing he was a stoner with no thoughts of the future—didn't even have his voicemail set up. God, I hoped she didn't end up with Bryce.

I called Molly again, this time leaving a message. "Hey, Molly, I hope that you and your family are well. Can you do me a favor and run down the hall to check in on Bridge? I wasn't able to get ahold of her this afternoon. Take care, sweetie."

After hanging up, I turned to Bridget's social media accounts, hoping to find a clue about her whereabouts. But there were no new posts or comments. The digital silence was deafening.

I called Kenny. I hated doing it. Every interaction led him either to ask me for money or ask me to take him back. But there was a chance she'd been in touch with him.

The phone barely made it through the first ring before he answered. "Macy? You need something?"

"Have you heard from Bridge?" I blurted out, my voice tight with worry.

Kenny paused, and I could almost hear the gears turning in his head. "Not today."

"She's not answering her phone and I'm starting to get worried."

"When was the last time you heard from her?"

"I got a voicemail from her earlier today but…"

"Oh, Macy, you are always thinking something terrible has

happened. You're overreacting. Remember the last time she didn't answer and you got super worried? She'd left her phone at a girlfriend's house and didn't bother to pick it up. You sent her twenty text messages and six voicemails in that forty-eight hours."

"Yeah," I said. "I remember." When we finally heard from her two days later, she told us she'd left the phone by accident then decided not to retrieve it because it seemed like a good time for a dopamine fast. "But Kenny, she told me she wouldn't scare me like that again."

"You know how she is," Kenny said. "Her phone charger probably died and she was too lazy or broke to get to the store and replace it."

Kenny was right, that did sound like our girl. It was probably nothing. Maybe this time she was taking an intentional digital time out and forgot to tell me. I just stayed silent and held the phone to my ear, unable to shake the worry despite all the reasons to be calm, my brain was shouting at me.

"She's a big girl now," Kenny said. "You have to let her live her life and not constantly hover. You know, the way you tend to do."

With those words, fueled by fear and frustration, my temper flared. "I know, I know, she's an adult. I guess I just want some reassurance that she's okay."

"Just chill, Mac," Kenny continued, activating his trademark lack of reassurance. "I mean, did you eat today? Maybe you're hungry."

Kenny had always been the cook in our relationship. I went from my mother's table to the dining hall at UW, to ordering takeout with Bruce, to Kenny's cooking, which while not four-star, was as reliable as a 7-11. And Kenny never left for longer than I could survive on peanut butter off a spoon. These days, I went to my mother's house for food a few times a week to make sure I was eating enough vegetables.

"Yes, I've eaten," I lied.

"Fine, but you're still overreacting. Don't be like one of those hysterical, nail biting helicopter parents."

Hysterical? Just what every woman *loves* to be called. Next he'd be asking me if my period was about to start. *None of his business,* but it probably was.

I'd finished my coffee and, with my frustration and rage bubbling over, I needed something a little stronger. I grabbed a cheap beer from the fridge and mixed it with some Bloody Mary mix. It needed a lime wedge I didn't have, but still, better than nothing.

Red Beer in hand, I stepped out onto the moonlit beach, the cool sand soothing my frazzled nerves.

"I'm not overreacting, Kenny." I took a deep breath of cool beach air, trying to ensure that my words came out calmer than they were sounding in my head. "I am simply concerned. I have a bad feeling and—"

"Oh, your *feelings*. A very reliable way to look at the world..."

That was it.

For the next ten minutes we argued back and forth. Old resentments bubbled to the surface and our conversation quickly devolved into a shouting match. Finally, I couldn't take it anymore and hung up on him, my hands shaking. I wished he would come back so I could run off to Florida instead and leave *him* to pick up the pieces of the parts of my life he'd detonated.

I sat down near the water's edge, sipping my drink and glancing back in the direction of the beach house. My grandmother had bought the place in the late forties when property here was dirt cheap. It was my sanctuary, the one thing I owned free and clear of Kenny, and I clung to it like a buoy in a typhoon.

As the waves lapped at my feet, I reflected on the tumultuous journey that led me to this moment. Tears welled in my eyes, spilling down my cheeks as the weight of the past days—the past year—finally broke me. I sobbed, my body wracked with the pain of fear and regret. The Salish Sea gave no indication it had noticed my suffering. Its vastness was both comforting and terrifying in its indifference.

In high school I'd been a competitive swimmer and at that moment I wanted to jump into the water and swim as far as I could. Instead I sat there in the sand, letting the salty taste of tears mingle with the briny sea air, searching for the happiness that had once been within reach. I surrendered myself to the grief that consumed me.

My mind finally went blank and all I could do was hold my red beer and cry. After I don't know how long I downed the rest of my drink and trudged back inside, rubbing my temples. Feeling utterly helpless, I collapsed onto the love seat in the living room area.

Sensing my distress, Gonzo padded over and nudged my leg with his cold, wet nose. I sighed and reached down and the dog somewhat reluctantly let me scritch his head. "What am I going to do, buddy?" I whispered, my voice cracking. "Where's my girl?"

Gonzo just licked and whined. When he wasn't whining he was licking, when he wasn't licking he was whining. When he couldn't decide if he should lick or whine, he did both and bit his tongue instigating more whining.

I once read that stopping a dog from licking you can make them feel rejected. But when his tongue felt dry against the back of my hand I tried to subtly block the licks to prevent him from dying of severe dehydration.

I noticed my hunger over the top of the cold coffee and beer and made my body move into the kitchen. I stood at the open fridge and ate a small dinner of carrots and deli-sliced turkey without utensils. I pulled out pieces enough for Gonzo, who jumped nervously onto the table and took a few sips of water from the little bowl I'd placed there for him. He whined, clearly expecting his dinner. I slowly fed Gonzo tiny bites until he jumped back down to find his taco nest. Sensing his day was done, he wiggled into his bed, licking his own paw once before going still and falling asleep.

I completed my bedtime routine and crawled into bed next to my baseball bat.

I WOKE up the next morning with my cell phone still in my hand.

No message from Bridget.

I called and it went straight to voicemail. I left her another message, trying and probably failing to sound calm and measured. Maybe she'd gone to that brunch and was now staying over with friends, or even that boy she'd said was cute.

I'd arranged to meet the crew back at the hospital first thing in the morning, and I managed to take Kenny's advice from the night before and suspend my worry long enough to execute morning tasks and make it out the door.

CHAPTER 37

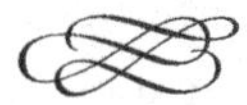

THE HOSPITAL in Seattle was a stark contrast to the cozy chaos of my beachfront home. Antiseptic smells filled the air, mingling with the scent of fear and sickness. The hallway was a flurry of activity—doctors and nurses rushing by, their polyester-blend scrubs swishing with every hurried step. Patients and visitors shuffled in and out of rooms, a never-ending parade of humanity.

I sat, anxiously waiting for news—either from Bridget or about Carlo.

Something, anything.

No matter how tightly I held my cell phone, Bridget had still not answered my calls or texts, and it had been a few hours since anyone heard anything about Carlo.

Next to me, Clint had his head buried in his hands, his usually confident demeanor replaced with a deep sense of guilt. He had gotten here three hours before me after two hours of sleep, and looked like he hadn't even gotten that. His blazer and slacks were wrinkled, his shoes still bore scrapes and scuffs marks from kneeling in the alley.

The sound of heels clicking against the linoleum floor

caught my attention and I looked up to see The Iron Chief, Jacqueline Bangor, striding toward us with purpose. Her steely gaze bore into us as she stopped in front of Clint and me, her anger palpable.

Without waiting for us to speak, she gritted her teeth and spat, "You got one of my people hit by a car. Now his leg hangs in jeopardy and three ribs are broken..." She paused, her eyes narrowing. "There's video on social media of you driving recklessly through traffic yesterday. You're embarrassing the WSP! You're lucky he's not dead and that I haven't killed you yet, Clint."

Clint tried to interrupt, to explain, but Jacqueline seemed to be able to freeze him with her look of quiet rage.

"Did they find Heath?" I blurted out, trying to change the subject and draw some of the heat from Clint.

She shook her head. "On top of everything else, Heath is in the wind."

I rubbed my forehead, feeling the weight of exhaustion bearing down on me.

Clint said, "Maria checked everywhere, and there are no other addresses he's associated with."

"And nothing from Jared, either," the Chief said. "You have two suspects, and they are both in the wind."

I let out a long sigh.

Clint opened his mouth to speak, then let his head fall back into his hands. "We screwed up," he said softly. "We'll fix it."

Nodding, Jacqueline stepped back, her professional demeanor returning. "Solve this thing today, Clint. Or do you feel like fetching lattes for the Feds?" With that, she turned on her 3-inch heels and marched away.

As the Chief disappeared down the hallway, Maria approached. She looked worn out, her eyes red and her clothes disheveled. Despite her fatigue, she shared some good news. "They were able to save his leg."

I wrapped my arm around her, offering what little comfort I could. "Thank God."

My own exhaustion threatened to consume me, and I struggled to keep my eyes open as Maria set next to me.

Then, a familiar voice cut through the haze. "There you are, honey."

I looked up, startled to see Kenny standing in the hallway. His sandy blonde hair was disheveled, and his face was drawn and weary, but he still managed to look handsome despite his obvious distress.

He strode directly toward me, ignoring everyone else. "Macy, I'm here."

He extended a hand full of flowers that I was sure he'd purchased from a gas station or stolen from a cemetery on his way to the hospital. Ignoring them, I grabbed his arm and led him down the hallway to a quiet corner next to the vending machines. "What the hell are you doing here, Kenny?"

He ran a hand through his hair, his blue eyes searching for mine. "I caught the red-eye from Florida right after you hung up on me. You sounded so worried last night I thought maybe I could help calm you down."

I clenched my fists, my voice rising. "I dare you to call me hysterical again."

He held up both hands. "I wouldn't dare."

"I'm at work right now. Your presence is *not* calming."

He scoffed, his face flushed with anger. "You think I don't care? I got on the first flight here when you called! Warrant or no warrant, I'm going to be there for my family, Mac. Have you heard from our daughter?"

"No. And I don't appreciate you using her not answering my texts for a day as a way to try to get back with me or whatever it is you're doing."

This was *soooo* Kenny.

Despite his flaws, he'd always tried to be a good husband and father. The problem was, he didn't know how. Time after time he'd screw everything up, then come running in with a grand, inappropriate gesture that fell far short. *Hey baby, I know I lost Bridge's college fund betting on the Seahawks, but I brought home a pizza! Mushroom and black olives—your favorite!!* His efforts were so wide of the mark it was often difficult to tell what he was aiming at in the first place.

He tried to hand me the flowers.

"No."

"What can I do?" Kenny pleaded.

"You know what you could have done if you were so worried about me worrying about our daughter? You could have driven straight to her apartment building and found her for me." I'd called Molly three more times and still hadn't heard back.

He just stood there in a stupor, looking down at the flowers.

"So, what's your plan now? What are you going to do, Kenny?"

"Have Frank drive me to Bremerton."

"Frank?"

"He's *not* that drunk right now," he said, sounding almost proud. "He's been cutting back and staying under .08. Drove to the airport to pick me up and he's in the roundabout waiting for me out front."

"Don't get me started about all the things that are wrong with this picture, Kenny." I thought of Frank down in the roundabout, only a little drunk, blocking sick people seeking medical assistance from entry and exit to the hospital.

"Do me a favor, if you do drive with Frank, you drive. I don't want to find our daughter and then have to tell her you're *dead*."

"You'll see, Mac. Bridget is just fine. Kids are all into dopamine fasts these days, right? Three days with no cellphone, all that jazz. Saw it on the news. Well, actually in a meme. But still, I'm here, and me and Frank are gonna go and find her for you." He spoke as he walked backwards, looking over his shoulder to make sure he had clearance.

I stood there until he turned the corner to the elevators.

"How the hell did he find me here?" I muttered.

"What was all that?" Maria said as I slumped down next to her.

"Gah! Just... my husband," I managed.

"I thought you two were split."

"We are."

"Oh," she said, sounding unconvinced.

"Here's the thing Maria," I said, my voice full of warning. "Choose wisely. If you raise a person with a person, that's it, you're glued for life."

"I'm a long way off from people making," Maria said.

"Yeah," I teased, "just how long does it take for a broken leg to heal, I wonder?"

My phone rang. *Molly*, Bridget's friend.

"Macy? It's Molly," her voice sounded distant.

"Did you get my messages? Have you seen Bridget?"

"I got them, and when she didn't show up for Pilates this morning I called around. She never made it to that brunch, either. I checked her apartment, no answer. Then I called security. Macy..." her voice cracked... "we think she's been abducted. They've got video surveillance from yesterday and... and they found her phone out front or something. Next to a spilled cake."

PART III
FINAL PROGNOSIS

CHAPTER 38

THE CONFERENCE ROOM at the office of the Washington State Patrol buzzed with a tense energy. Clint and Maria were there, along with Katya, the tech-savvy member of our team. I took my seat, my body aching from the sleepless night, but I had to be strong and focused.

The grainy surveillance video from the side of the apartment building appeared to show Bridget being led by a man at gunpoint. The video had captured them for only a few seconds before they went out of view. It was impossible to tell who the man was—his face was blocked by a hooded sweatshirt—but his height, and something about the way he moved, made me think of Jared.

I cursed Kenny for gaslighting what turned out to be my mothering instincts trying to warn me that my daughter was in danger. But, even louder, I cursed myself for not doing more to follow my gut. How could I have been so easily swayed from hearing the *mother's intuition* that had practically been screaming at me through a bullhorn since yesterday?

Clint came in looking frazzled. "Alright, everyone. Let's go over what we know." He took charge of the meeting as the late morning sun seeped through the blinds, casting a harsh glow across the room.

I struggled to hold myself together. This wasn't the time for tears or self-pity; I needed to find my daughter.

"Carlo is still in the hospital, but he's expected to make a full recovery," Clint began. "You all have seen the video. Macy's daughter is missing. She's been abducted and we're treating this as a connected case."

I gritted my teeth, my mind racing with relentless worst-case story lines.

"Campus security is working with local police to question everyone around the school, including her classmates and the people she often had lunch with," Clint continued. "Unfortunately, security footage is not clear enough to distinguish her captor. But, obviously, Jared and Heath are at the top of our list."

"Looks like Jared to me," I said.

Clint held up a hand. "It *could* be Jared. But we have to keep an open mind. Heath is still missing. But, Macy, your husband showed up out of nowhere with Frank, a well-known drunk who's lived on the edge of the law and..."

"There's no way Kenny is involved in this. He'd run into a burning building for Bridget." I considered what I'd just said. "Decent chance he would have *started* the fire by accident, but he'd run in nonetheless. Plus, he came *after* she disappeared."

"Okay," Clint said, "but we'll want to confirm that. Call him?"

I glanced over at Maria, who sat slumped in her chair, her eyes red from exhaustion. We were all running on empty, but we couldn't afford to stop.

"Got it," I said.

I dialed and Kenny answered right away. "We're on our way, Mac, another ten minutes until we get to the campus."

"Do you have me on speaker phone?" I asked. In the past, Kenny had often neglected to tell me when he had me on speaker phone. Sometimes his buddies overheard our conversations. Worse, sometimes customers at The Wrench King got detailed information about our personal lives. More than once I got a call from my mother, who'd heard from someone in the neighborhood, who had heard from someone at the shop, that Kenny had pissed away a large sum of money again.

"No," he said. "What's up?"

"Pull over. Get on your phone and email me your flight receipt, boarding pass, whatever. I need to show the cops you aren't involved in Briget's disappearance."

"What?" he shouted. "Disappearance?"

"Just do it. I know you're not… look, Kenny, there's no time to explain. Bridget is missing. Taken. Do what I say, then get to her apartment and start looking everywhere, talking to everyone. Find out if anyone saw her with a man."

I hung up without another word. He knew as well as I did that I was better in a crisis, and I had no doubt he'd follow my orders.

Clint had just ended a call of his own. "Tacoma PD. Heath didn't go back to his apartment or office last night. No one knows where he is. He would have had enough time to drive to Bremerton and may be responsible for Bridget's abduction."

"Still think the body type looked a lot like Jared," I said.

Maria looked over at me and asked quietly, "Is there any chance, however remote, that Kenny may have had something to do with Bridget's disappearance? Like a way to get you back together with him or something? I had a boyfriend once who—"

"No way," I said. I couldn't bring myself to think about that possibility. "Kenny is a degenerate gambler and might go to great lengths to try to get me back. But messing with our daughter would be going too far, even for him."

Maria stood up, pacing the room as her mind worked overtime. Finally, she spoke. "As I was waiting to hear about Carlo, I spent most of the night going through old case files from the Seattle PD—the original Waxlace Strangler case. Definitely looks like a shoddy investigation. Jared was clearly disturbed, and they settled on him way too early. Maybe they're somehow in on it together? Jared and Heath, I mean."

The room fell silent as we all considered the possibility. It seemed far-fetched, but a possibility. My thoughts were muddled. Truth was, with Bridget missing, I no longer cared about anything else.

"Find any connection between Jared and Heath, no matter how small," Clint said, breaking the silence. "We can't leave any stone unturned."

"I can run some algos," Katya said. "See if I get any pings in the public records that connect them."

My phone chimed with a text message—a receipt from Kenny's flight purchase, which he made thirty minutes after I'd called him about Bridget. Holding it up to Clint, I said, "Can we drop him as a suspect? This was *after* I called him about our daughter."

Clint nodded. "For now at least, yeah. I trust you."

"Maybe Jared's got something on Heath," Maria suggested, her brow furrowed in thought. "He could be using it as leverage to make Heath do his bidding."

"Or Heath could be working with Jared willingly," Katya chimed in. "He might have his own reasons for wanting to be involved."

As the conversation continued, Clint's patience seemed to wear thin. He slammed his hand down on the table, silencing the room. "Our job is to find them both. We can figure out who did what later."

With the room quiet, I stood up and began to pace, my legs tense from sitting too long. I stared out the window, thoughts swirling in my head. I needed to look closer.

I needed to notice everything.

An idea struck me, and I turned back to the group. "Maria,

those files? Do you have ones from Jared's time in the psychiatric prison?"

Maria looked puzzled. "I do, but why would you want those? I've been focused on the ones from the original case."

"Email them to me," I said, my eyes locked on hers.

Maria's confusion was evident, but Clint nodded his approval. She pulled out her phone and tapped a few buttons. "Everything I have, you now have."

An email notification popped up on my phone, and I retreated to a corner of the room. Sitting cross-legged on the floor, I began scrolling through hundreds of pages of documents. There was one thing in particular I was looking for, one detail that might make all the difference.

As I read, I could hear the others resume their conversation, their voices low and urgent. But their words were just background noise as I focused, my mind racing with possibilities. The answer had to be in there somewhere, hidden among the records of Jared's time in that psychiatric prison.

I was determined to find the answers.

And my Bridget.

CHAPTER 39

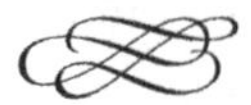

SITTING cross-legged in the corner of the office, the hum of conversation from the detectives faded into the background. My focus was entirely on the reports on Jared's mental health from the psychiatric hospital.

As I scrolled frantically through the documents, I thought about the article I'd written twenty years ago, suggesting that some members of the police believed Jared wasn't the killer. For twenty years, Jared stewed on that article. He'd told me I was his only hope. He'd imagined me to be some sort of crusader, on his side. In truth, I'd just been a young, inexperienced reporter trying to keep my job so I could pay down my student loans.

My gut had told me that Jared was innocent of the murders. And the evidence had confirmed that. But now… now I suspected he'd taken Bridget. Why? What were we missing?

Something Maria had said started a train of thought. What if, somehow, they were working together. That all along we'd been looking for one suspect when really we should have been looking for two?

Assuming he was innocent of the Waxlace Strangler murders, Jared had spent two decades locked up for crimes he hadn't committed. Already psychologically fragile, that twenty years would have been torture.

Perhaps the whole time he'd been waiting to get out, to get his revenge. If his rambling during our interview had shown anything, it was that he'd believed Heath to be the killer all along. So there was a twisted logic to wanting revenge on Heath. Was it somehow possible that, when he'd gotten out, he'd killed Cara, somehow attempting to frame Heath?

Or, oh, God.

I don't know why or how, but my gut landed on an even stranger conclusion, one that somehow fit with what I knew of Jared.

What if he'd somehow *forced* Heath to come to Hansville and kill Cara?

I sighed, rubbing my temples.

That would explain the call I received. The call the police received.

Perhaps Jared had chosen Hansville because he'd learned that *I* lived there. In his twisted mind, he'd believed that I was on his side, that I'd write a story about the real killer. That we'd catch Heath as he tried to kill Cara, thereby proving that Jared was innocent all along.

When I'd let him down, he'd taken the thing that mattered to me most.

Bridget.

It was possible, but how could he have gotten Heath to kill Cara?

I shook my head. I was still missing something.

I was almost sure the man in the video was Jared. So, for now, the important thing to figure out was where he'd taken my daughter.

Clint had coordinated with Seattle police, confirming that Jared had not returned to his apartment. He hadn't returned to the diner, or the library. In fact, no one had seen him since he'd been released after Clint and I interviewed him.

"He wasn't rich," I muttered. "Didn't have a second home, but somehow he has access to somewhere he feels safe."

My hands trembled as I continued poring over Jared's records, my heart pounding with the certainty that he had taken Bridget *somewhere*. I needed to find where, and fast. As I examined each document, I stumbled on his visitation records for the past year.

Scanning frantically, I looked for names I knew from the case and the trial. He hadn't had many visitors.

Only three names stood out on the list. One was his court-appointed attorney. Another was his mother, who'd passed away two years ago. The last one I didn't recognize: *Karen McFadden*.

Clutching the paper, I hurried over to Katya. "Find me every address associated with her," I urged, my voice tight with anxiety. "And anything else you can."

She nodded, her eyes dancing toward her twin laptops on the desk, and went to work.

CHAPTER 40

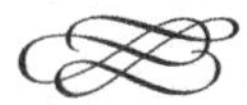

COUNTLESS STUFFED birds fill the small cabin, their glassy eyes holding distant blank stares. The cabin is far from luxurious. Its dusty windows let in little light. Jared stands in the center of the room, observing the frightened girl he has tied to a wooden post.

His gaze settles on her. Mouth sealed with duct tape, she says nothing, but her eyes speak volumes. They plead with him, full of fear and confusion.

"Do you like birds?" he asks her, his voice melodic and raspy, like a poet consumed by madness. The girl hesitates, unsure of how to respond, before giving a small nod.

"Good," he says, his speech shifting between eloquent phrases and disjointed words, "for they are my friends, my precious ones. Can you see them? The swans, the eagles, the tiny sparrows... all here, all preserved for eternity."

Jared's eyes gleam with a feverish intensity as he shares his passion for the birds, recounting their names.

"I once had a dream, you know," he confesses, momentarily lost in his memories. "Twenty years ago, I danced upon the ice, like a bird in flight. I dreamed of the Olympics, the glory, the applause."

"But my father... he called me names for loving to skate." His face contorts with pain as he recalls this dark memory. "Said if I skate but don't play hockey, he has no use for me as a son. My mother, she supported me, but he... he broke me. And not just by way of beatings."

Tears stream down Jared's face, but he quickly wipes them away, resuming his ramblings. "Do you know how many types of birds there are?"

She doesn't reply.

"I thought your mom was the one who believed in me when they decided I killed those girls." He leans in closer, his voice trembling. "I didn't kill anyone. Never have. Do you believe me?"

The girl nods vigorously.

His eyes fall upon the girl's gray hoodie and the words printed in cursive catch his attention: *Notice Everything*. "Is that a custom print?" he inquires, gesturing to the words.

The girl nods in response.

He furrows his brow, clearly intrigued by the phrase. *Notice everything*.

Leaning down, he slowly peels back the duct tape. Only half-way, ensuring she can breathe, but not scream. His voice a mix of curiosity and caution, he asks, "What does it mean?"

"It's my mom's..." Her voice trembles like the shaky, warbling trill of a Blue-winged Teal duck. "I don't know. It's like a saying or something...."

Jared's eyes narrow and he quickly reseals her mouth with the duct tape. "Do you really believe me?" He studies her face for a moment before posing another question. "That I never killed anyone?"

The panic in her eyes intensifies, and she nods aggressively, desperately.

"I've never killed anyone," he says. "But if they think I'm a killer, my only option is to be a killer. If they locked me away for something I didn't do, if they don't admit my innocence, I can't *remain* innocent. That wouldn't make sense. I will have to kill. To make things right."

From a nearby table, he retrieves a cheap disposable cell-phone encased in hard plastic. As he dials a number, the girl's eyes widen in horror, her heart pounding in her chest.

"First," Jared says, his voice the menacing screech of a red-tailed hawk, "let's make a little call and give her one last chance."

CHAPTER 41

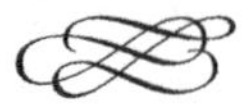

MY PHONE RANG. An unfamiliar number flashed across the screen and a cold dread settled in my stomach. I hesitated, took a deep breath, and answered, "Hello?"

"Hello, Macy," the voice on the other end was thin and screechy.

I realized who it was immediately. *Jared.*

All eyes in the room landed on me as I hit the speaker button so others could hear.

"Do you have Bridget?" I demanded, struggling to keep the fear out of my voice.

"I will let her go once you publish an article that tells the world I'm innocent," he replied, his tone as unnerving as his words, "and once the police go on TV and *say* I'm innocent."

My mind raced, panic boiling over as I clenched my fists. I glanced at Clint, who subtly shook his head, urging me not to give in. "Jared," I said, my voice wavering. "We know about Heath. We found him and he ran. We're trying to catch him right now. You don't have to do this. You're going to be *proven* innocent when we catch him."

"Oh, but I'm *not* innocent," Jared's voice sent chills down my spine. "I took the girls. I ripped them from their nests like I had been ripped from mine. I kept them in a cage. One I let fly free. The one you know may not be so lucky."

He was talking about Bridget. But who was the other girl? The one he'd let *fly free*?

Clint stepped forward and took the phone from me. "Jared, this is Detective Captain Clinton McKenna. Macy is right; we know about Heath. We know he was at the ice rink. We know about the wax laces from the ice skates. He's going to be in our custody soon, and the truth will come out. You don't have to keep Bridget."

Jared was silent for a moment, then chuckled darkly. "You think it's that simple?"

"Macy believes you're innocent," Clint countered, his voice steady. "And she's been fighting to prove it. Don't throw that away. You can still come out of this without blood on your hands."

The line went silent for a few agonizing seconds before Jared spoke again, his voice low and threatening. "You have the rest of the day to prove it. Make me believe you're on my side, and maybe I set your little song bird free."

The line went dead.

My legs gave out beneath me, and I collapsed into a nearby chair, my body wracked with sobs.

Maria hurried over and pulled me back up. "Macy, c'mon. You've got this."

I stood, leaning on a wall, listening to my own breath as I tried to regain my composure.

I glanced at Katya every few seconds as she furiously typed and scanned two laptops at once. The ticking clock in my head reminded me that Bridget's safety was slipping away with each passing second.

Finally, Katya looked up. "Got something."

My heart leaped into my throat and I hurried over to her. "What did you find?"

Katya explained that Karen McFadden was Jared's mother's brother's ex-wife. Though she was no longer related to Jared by marriage, it seemed she had stayed close to him, or perhaps just felt sorry for him. Other than doctors, psychologists, lawyers, and his mother, she'd been the only person to visit him regularly. A former amateur figure skater who never made it to the Olympics, Karen had died a year ago, leaving behind a cabin south of Seattle that bordered the Collinswood Nature Preserve and Bird Sanctuary.

I felt a spark of realization ignite in my mind.

Bird Sanctuary.

I turned to Clint. "Jared was reading that book about birds in the library and kept talking about birds." My pulse quickened. "Jared is there."

Clint raised a hand to slow me down. "Not so fast," he said. His brow furrowed as he turned to Katya. "I mean, who lives there? Did she leave it to anyone in her will? What's the deal with the property?"

Katya's fingers flew across the keyboard. "Currently, it's in probate. I don't see a copy of her will, but legally she still owns the place. It's very possible Jared knows about it and is hiding out there."

The room fell silent as everyone absorbed the information. A glimmer of hope flickered in my chest, but I knew we had to act fast. I looked at Clint, my eyes pleading. "We have to go now. If there's even a chance Bridget is there..."

Clint nodded, his expression grim. "It's only twenty minutes away. Maria, Macy, you ride with me. I'll call for backup on the way to the car."

CHAPTER 42

INSIDE THE CABIN, he stares at Bridget, his little passerine. She remains tied to a chair, wrapped up in duct tape. Her mouth held shut, she's unable to sing. Her wings held down, she's unable to fly.

His thoughts swirl, a mix of madness and twisted logic.

"Little Budgie," he croons, his voice slipping into the smooth tones of a doting uncle. "So out of place here in the Pacific Northwest, far from your native Australia."

He repeats the name "Budgie," his voice slipping between the cracks of his fractured mind. "Do you believe me, little Budgie? Please, believe me. It isn't me," he pleads, his voice strained with desperation.

But then a switch flips inside him, his voice turns dark. "I thought your mother believed me," he spits, his eyes wild with rage. "But she was a dirty bird, a pigeon. A vulture dressed in swan feathers! I thought she was a Japanese white-eye." His voice wavers, becoming almost lyrical. "But instead, she's a parrot who learned to speak from a sailor. Dirty-mouthed, dirty bird. Sneaky birdie, a tricky, deceptive, and manipulative bird."

His little bird moans underneath the duct tape.

"Like a forked-tailed drongo," he continues, "tricking and scaring good birds like me." His eyes narrow, his voice dripping with disdain. "A common cuckoo who would lay her eggs in another bird's nest, too lazy to raise her own chicks, a cheat and a loafing liar." His voice shifts back to a sickly sweet sing-song. "But I'm smart, and now I have her little chick tied up and—"

What is his little bird looking at. Her groans have stopped. Her eyes have shifted, gone wide in fear, or surprise.

Have they come for him?

He turns to see what has captured the attention of his little chickie.

A sharp blow strikes his head. He crumples to the floor.

Looking up, he sees a silver gleam, a blade. A skating blade. Behind it, the smiling face of Heath.

Heath kneels, tugs the blade along his throat. "I know you've been looking for your skates." His cruelty and deep croaking voice are like a Raven.

Jared reaches up. A trickle of blood on his neck. He hears the skates dropping to the floor with a heavy thud.

His thoughts scatter like a flock of frightened geese.

CHAPTER 43

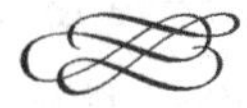

CLINT DROVE us down a winding dirt road, the dense forest crowding in on either side.

Maria sat in the passenger seat, gripping the handle nervously.

Sitting in the back, I spotted a sign for a bird sanctuary, my heart pounding. A moment later, I spotted the cabin, old and dilapidated, up a gentle slope about a hundred yards away. A patrol car was parked at a curve behind overgrown blackberry bushes that blocked half the road and the view of the car from the cabin.

"State troopers," Clint said, his voice tense. "Got here five minutes ago. I told them not to approach until we arrived."

As we rolled up behind the patrol car, Clint lowered the window and exchanged a few hushed words with the officers. Then he got out, followed by Maria.

I tried to open the door. No dice, safety locks had been set.

Clint turned when he heard me knock on the window.

I pointed towards the car door handle, gesturing for him to let me out.

"Stay in the car," he said. Clint's tone allowed for no rebuttal, but I cracked the window—the two inches it allowed—so I could listen in.

Huddled outside the car, Clint stood in a group with Maria and the two other officers. "Alright, here's the plan. Maria, you and Officer Adams will approach from the front, staying low and using the trees for cover. Officer Banks and I will circle around to the back. We'll move in slowly. Weapons ready, be prepared for anything. If Jared is there, we need to make sure we've got all possible exits covered. Communication is key. If anyone spots Jared or Bridget, use your radios and let the others know. We can't afford any mistakes."

Everyone nodded in agreement, the tension in the air palpable.

Clint locked eyes with me, his expression deadly serious. "I let you come along because your daughter is missing. If the Chief finds out I let you come, I'm dead. And if you leave this car, I'll shoot you myself."

I swallowed hard, nodding my understanding.

I had to trust them to do their jobs, even though every fiber of my being wanted to rush in after them and curl Bridget into my arms to shield her from danger. But a mother's love wouldn't offer the kind of protection she needed right now.

As Clint, Maria, and the two officers slowly approached the house, I remained in the car, watching their progress with bated breath.

Gripping the door handle so tightly my knuckles turned white, I prayed to anyone who might be out there listening that they would find Bridget safe and sound.

The seconds ticked by like hours, each step they took reverberated and sent a wave that made my heart pound with every footfall.

After a minute, they were no longer in view. They'd taken a gentle curve and disappeared behind a cedar tree.

CHAPTER 44

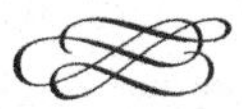

THE PAIN in his head is intense and he struggles to make sense of the situation.

As he lies there, his vision blurred, he expects stars and tiny birds to circle like in the cartoons.

He doesn't see either and is especially crestfallen that there aren't any birds when he looks up.

All he sees is Heath. Looming over him, Heath's voice cuts through the fog in his mind. "I can't go home, can't go to my work. Soon I'll be gone, but I needed to make one last stop." He kicks the skates toward Jared and they skid to a stop next to his head. "When they find your body, they'll find the skates I used all those years ago."

"Please..." Jared manages.

"You never should have brought my daughter here," Heath continues. "Twenty years, and that was the best idea you could come up with?"

"Please..."

"But I'm glad you did. I liked killing Cara, just as I'm going to like killing... what's this one's name?"

Jared can't speak. He's bleeding out.

"Kid, you got me hooked," Heath drawls, grinning wickedly. "I came here to take care of *you*, Jared, to leave the skates. But it's like you brought me this gift. I'd forgotten the thrill of the strangle. The youthful energy being slowly drained as the waxed lace slips tighter and tighter. Those girls didn't live long after refusing me twenty years ago. Cara never had the opportunity to refuse me in the first place. Neither will this one. When I leave here, I'll have whoever finds you thinking you killed again and took your unbalanced life with your own depraved hands."

Jared's thoughts twist and turn, grappling with the reality of Heath's presence. He wants to be the one in control, the puppet master pulling the strings, but now he's at the mercy of someone even more dangerous and unpredictable than himself.

"This one isn't for you," he manages to squeak out, weak as a baby chick. "She's not for that."

The room closes in on him as Heath moves around the room, his shadow dominating Jared's vision, the cruel twist of fate leaving him as trapped and helpless as the little passerine he had captured.

Jared looks up when he hears a quiet snap.

Heath is slipping a long shoelace between his fingers, meticulously preparing for his sinister purpose.

His vision is still sideways and hazy from the blow to his head, but he can't tear his eyes away from the lace, so new, so shiny and waxy, like the ones from so long ago.

His head throbs with pain, the room spinning and shifting as he struggles to make sense of the chaos.

Through his disoriented gaze, Jared observes the room in disjointed fragments: the windows, distorted and warped; Heath's expensive leather shoes, polished to a gleaming shine; Bridget's whimpering, barely audible through the duct tape over her mouth and the ringing in his ears, are the pitiful cries of a small, injured bird.

His precious green and teal skates… if only he were close enough to reach them. He'd like that, to be holding them on his way out of this world.

Heath steps closer to Bridget, wrapping the shoelace around her neck with deliberate care. As he begins to pull it tight, his head jerks back. A noise outside catches his attention.

Boots on gravel, perhaps.

"No matter," Heath mutters. "I'll enjoy this more if it's done privately. C'mon little lady, looks like I'll need you for a hostage. "

With a vicious yank, Heath pulls out a pocket knife and cuts Bridget loose from the chair.

Jared tries to reach for his skates, but his body won't cooperate.

Instead, he watches. His focus vacillates between his skates in the foreground and Heath in the background. He's pulling the girl out through the back door, dragging her into the heavy woods of the bird sanctuary.

Still sprawled on the floor, Jared sees them disappear into the wilderness, his vision blurring further until they seem to transform into birds taking flight.

His senses dim.

The room disappears into darkness.

His consciousness becomes feathers on the wind.

CHAPTER 45

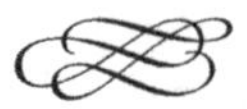

I SAT in the back of the police car, feeling as though I was suffocating in the silence. The air was different here, drier and less damp than the salty air by the beach back home. I could smell the trees, the earthy scent of the forest, dirt, moss, and the delicate aroma of decaying pine needles.

Staring out the window up the dirt road, waiting, listening for gunshots I hoped wouldn't come, I'd have done anything to have the life I had before, even if it meant taking Kenny back. At least then, Bridget would be safe.

As that thought passed through my mind, my gaze flicked to the rearview mirror. I froze, breath catching in my chest.

What the?

Standing twenty yards behind the car was a figure. A man's back to me. He turned slowly.

What the actual hell?

It was Kenny.

My heart flushed warm for a moment, my sense of time skewed and I felt as though none of this nightmare was real. We were back on the beach, watching our baby girl lean over tide-pools to marvel at the barnacles. She'd watch them as they waved their showgirl-like white feathery cirri, then dance her hands through the water to watch them close their rooftop hatches. Kenny and I would furl and unfurl our fingers over our heads to imitate them, which always made Bridget laugh and laugh.

We all would laugh. We were happy there and then.

The rush of nostalgia was quickly replaced by a surge of anger.

What was Kenny doing here?

For half a second I wondered whether Clint had been right to be suspicious of Kenny. After all, he'd run an elaborate scheme to steal medications from my patients. He could have faked a flight receipt or gotten Frank to abduct her before picking him up at the airport. But it didn't make sense. He was *behind* me, far from the cabin, and Bridget was nowhere in sight.

He hadn't seen me in the car. My body snapped into motion. The car's back door was locked, and I couldn't unlock it from where I sat. Panic bubbled up in my chest, but I pushed it down and scrambled between the front seats, quietly opening the driver's side door and stepping out into the cool forest air. I didn't bother closing the door behind me. I was too focused on confronting Kenny.

I inched silently towards him. The anger I felt simmered beneath the surface, and threatened to boil over. As I drew closer, I took a deep breath, willing myself to stay calm. Finally, when I was a few yards away, I whispered, "What are you doing here, Kenny? What have you done?"

Kenny turned, fists raised. He dropped his shoulders when he saw it was me. "What do you mean, what have I done?" he whispered back, his tone full of accusation and tension that rivaled my own.

"Kenny, did you have something to do with Bridget going missing?"

"No. You know I had nothing to do… Wait. Where is she?"

"There's a cabin." I pointed up the driveway.

Kenny took a step toward it. "Why aren't you in there saving our daughter?"

I grabbed his arm. "The experts are handling it, Kenny." I clenched my fists, struggling to keep my composure. "I don't know the first thing about suspect apprehension, and neither do you. And we don't know for sure that she's in there."

As we stood, the sounds of the forest filled the air around us, birds, rustling leaves, the occasional moan of a tree shifting under its own weight, its trunk like a spine working to maintain its upright posture.

"How did you even know where I was?" I asked, my curiosity momentarily overriding my anger.

"I tracked your phone," he admitted sheepishly, a hint of pride creeping into his voice. "Frank and I went to Bridge's apartment and..." he shook his head... "anyway, I left Frank at the bar and came here."

Damnit. The *family* plan.

When we'd first gotten Bridget a phone, Kenny demanded that we add location tracking to it. I guess I shouldn't have been surprised that tracking included my phone, too. In paying to have the phone turned back on, I had inadvertently paid for *his* phone as well.

"You're a real bastard, Kenny." To my surprise, I leaned in and pressed my head against his jean jacket, which smelled of motor oil and coconut shampoo. "But I'm glad you're here."

The dense foliage and tall trees cast dappled shadows on the ground. I reflected on the frustrating paradox that was Kenny. He could be so infuriatingly clueless, and yet, there was a part of my heart that stubbornly refused to let go of the love I still felt for him. At that moment, I wished the loving-him part of my heart could be surgically removed like liposuction. A surgical procedure for the heart. A little nip and tuck eliminating my Kenny-shaped emotional love handles once and for all.

"They're up there now?" he asked.

"Yeah." I stepped back, positioning myself between Kenny and the rustic, wooden structure preventing him from going closer.

Kenny craned his neck, desperate to get a view into the structure to look for our Bridget. Then, jumping to the left, he jogged toward the cabin.

"Wait," I called, running after him.

He kept going, ten yards toward the cabin, then twenty. I saw a flash of black to my left.

"Kenny!" I screamed. "That's our baby."

Emerging from the woods I saw Heath, dragging Bridget roughly behind him, her mouth and hands bound with duct tape.

My mind raced, trying to make sense of the situation. *What the hell was Heath doing there?* I glanced toward the cabin. *Where were Clint and the others?*

Kenny stopped, turned. That's when I noticed the gun tucked into the waist of his jeans.

Heath pulled Bridget down a barely perceptible overgrown logging road that led to the cabin from another direction.

Kenny and I locked eyes for an instant, then raced after them, Kenny taking the lead.

I recognized Heath's Porsche immediately. Its sleek, black exterior contrasted sharply with the natural surroundings, almost as much as the gashes slashed down the side of it from its narrow escape after running over Carlo.

The car had been out of view from where I was sitting in the police cruiser. It was also out of view of Clint and the others when they approached the cabin. Heath must have come to the cabin via this frontage road.

The same road he would use to escape with Bridget.

CHAPTER 46

EVERY MUSCLE in my body was tense, ready to spring into action. I could feel my heart striking against my chest, my breaths coming in short, shallow gasps. The situation felt surreal, as if I were watching a nightmare unfold before my eyes. But this was no dream. This was real, and my daughter's life was hanging in the balance.

Heath dragged Bridget through the underbrush, her small frame struggling against his vice-like grip.

Reaching the Porsche, he opened the door, glancing at us.

Kenny and I bolted towards the vehicle, Kenny pulling out his gun as he ran.

Heath pushed Bridget through the driver's door, then squeezed himself in next to her, his weight pressing against her small frame. He had the door half closed when Kenny, gun in hand, came up beside the car. "Freeze!" Kenny shouted.

Heath's reaction was swift and brutal. He shoved the car door open with a violent thrust, slamming it into Kenny's chest and midsection. Kenny let out a groan, stumbled, then tripped backwards and fell to the ground. His head hit a rock, splattering crimson droplets on the dirt road. The gun flew into the underbrush.

My heart raced, panic and anger surging through me.

With Heath leaning halfway out the car, Bridget leaned away, reared up her feet, and kicked, managing to shove Heath out of the driver's side door and onto the ground.

Kicking and writhing, she slid down the driver's seat, finally landing on the floor of the vehicle, her legs poised to kick him away again should he try to make his way back in. The waxed shoelace still hung from her neck, its tail swinging back and forth like a macabre pendulum.

I scrambled for the gun, my wrists and forearms slashed by blackberry thorns.

I heard Heath groan.

My hand touched cold metal and I gripped the weapon.

As I turned, Bridget swung the door, striking Heath in the head as he tried to stand.

Darting toward the car, my back to my daughter, I pressed the cold metal barrel against Heath's temple, my voice trembling but determined. "I will shoot you. Nobody messes with my daughter."

He moved slightly, tilting his head toward me.

"Don't move again," I commanded. "I *will* shoot you."

"No you won't," Heath said, his voice smooth and sickening, like rancid oil. "I hear your fingers trembling."

My hand steadied as I slowly pulled back the hammer of the gun.

I had devoted myself to the nursing profession, following in the footsteps of my mother and her mother and my great grandmother, and raised Bridget to become the fifth generation nurse in our family. But the memories of Heath's victims, the four young lives he had stolen, gnawed at my conscience.

Could I really take a life?

I heard Bridget's gentle sobs coming from behind me and I

felt my resolve harden. I thought of Gonzo, of how he'd growl and snap at anyone who came too close to his territory.

This was my territory.

I was prepared to fight with the ferocity of a neurotic chihuahua mix to protect my daughter. The gun was heavy but the trigger felt so easy to pull. "Don't try me."

There was a long silence. Then, slowly, as though sensing my determination, Heath held up his hands defensively. "I was saving her from Jared," he stammered, trying to sound convincing. "I was saving her from Jared."

The wind rustled through the trees around us, the sound eerily reminiscent of a whispered warning. I glanced around, taking in every detail of the scene in slow motion—the way the leaves danced in the breeze, the shadows that stretched across the forest floor, and the fear etched on Heath's face.

"You're a liar," I spat, my voice dripping with contempt. "You're a monster, Heath, and I won't let you hurt my daughter. Or any other girl. Ever again."

My finger hovered over the trigger, every fiber of my being urging me to squeeze it, to put an end to the nightmare that had consumed our lives. But a small, nagging voice in the back of my mind whispered to me, insisting caution, reminding me that I needed to be sure, absolutely sure, before I took such an irreversible step.

Heath continued to plead, his voice a whimper. "Please, Macy, I didn't do it. I swear."

I looked into his eyes, searching for a hint of the truth, and found nothing but fear and desperation. It was then that I made my decision, feeling the weight of the responsibility settle onto my shoulders like a leaden cloak.

I took a deep breath, steadied my hand, and prepared to make a choice that would change our lives forever.

CHAPTER 47

"We got him, Mac." Clint's voice startled me, breaking through the tension like a sudden clap of thunder. "We got him. Hold your fire."

I allowed my eyes to find him. Clint stood next to Maria. Both had guns aimed at Heath's chest.

"Now, give me the gun," Clint said. "Macy, back up now."

My hands loosened, then regripped the gun.

"We got him," Clint urged. "You don't want Bridget to see this. Give us the gun and go to your girl."

I hesitated for a moment, still pointing the gun at Heath. Then, strangely, I thought of Gonzo. His little snarling growl, his tiny, sharp teeth. Given the choice, Gonzo would have killed Heath there and then, but I wouldn't.

I lowered the gun to the ground and allowed Clint to take it from my hands. The adrenaline that had been coursing through me suddenly evaporated, leaving me feeling weak and shaky. I collapsed to the ground, scrambling toward Bridget, releasing sighs and whimpers that sounded more animal than human.

I removed the duct tape from Bridget's mouth, but she didn't speak. I fumbled in my cellphone wallet case, pulling out the

Swiss Army card I always carried with me. My fingers trembled as I unfurled the tiny knife, carefully using it to slice through the duct tape around her wrists. I tried to keep my voice calm and soothing as I cooed to her. "See, it's okay. It's alright. We're okay now."

As the tape fell away, Bridget looked at me with tear-filled eyes. "Mom, please take care of dad."

I glanced over at Kenny, who was slowly stirring on the ground. He had a gash on the side of his head where it had struck the rock. I hurried to his side. He blinked at me, disoriented, as he sat up.

As Maria cuffed Heath and led him away, I leaned in to assess the wound, my nurse's instincts kicking in despite the chaos of the situation. Blood had splattered across his face, but the gash seemed less severe than I'd initially thought.

I tore a sleeve from his shirt, the fabric ripping with a satisfying sound. I wrapped it around Kenny's head, applying pressure to his wound. Blood seeped through the thin material, but it was enough to stop it from continuing to drip into his eyes.

I looked at him and said, "We got our girl, Kenny."

He met my gaze and, with a rare sincerity in his voice, replied, "*You* got our girl, Mac. I love you."

I couldn't help but smile. "Well, I did have a little help from your gun." A piece of me still wanted to scream at him for a dozen things at once, but what I heard myself saying was, "I love you too, Kenny."

Before long, paramedics and other police personnel arrived at the scene. They quickly attended to Jared, Heath, and Kenny. Jared, it turned out, had gotten the worst of it. As far as we could tell, Heath had arrived with the skates and cut him in the throat, intending to leave him to bleed out. When Clint and the others had stormed the cabin, Jared was unconscious, but alive. They'd followed his directions out the back and through the forest, but lost Heath's trail when he looped back toward the road.

Finally, Clint came up to us, a sad, awkward look across his face. "Kenny, you know there are warrants out for you, right?"

"I know," Kenny said, touching his head gingerly. The paramedics had given him a proper bandage, and, if I knew Kenny, he was going to try to milk it to get out of what was coming next.

"I have to take you in," Clint said.

"C'mon," Kenny said, "I... just let me..." he shook his head sadly, as though he'd finally grown tired of his own BS. "Do you need to cuff me?"

Clint took him by the arm. "That won't be necessary."

As Clint led him away, Kenny called out to me, "Hey, Macy, when I get out on bail, any chance you'd let me take you out to dinner?"

THAT NIGHT, I sat on the curb in front of the station, arm around Bridget, my heart swelling with a mix of relief and concern. She'd been through so much. But it was finally over.

I glanced over at Carlo, who wheeled in front of us, his leg outstretched on the wheelchair footrest in a cast. He'd just gotten out of the hospital. "Looking good, Carlo," I said, trying to lighten the mood. "How did you get them to let you out so soon?"

"They couldn't stop me," Carlo replied with a grin. "I had to be here."

I smiled back, but my focus quickly shifted to Bridget. She looked traumatized, felt distant, and I wished I could take all her pain away. My heart ached for her, but at the same time, I was overjoyed to have my daughter back in my arms. I grabbed her hand and gave it a quick double squeeze which she returned.

The squeeze was a gesture we had always done to check in with each other. The first double squeeze meant *are we good?* The second double squeeze meant *yeah, we're good.* When Bridget was a pre-teen she went through a period where she would never return a double squeeze and would often not be willing to even hold my hand. When she turned eighteen or nineteen, she came back around and decided she needed her mother again.

She needed me now more than ever.

Clint came out from the lobby and motioned for us to follow him to the office. As we walked, I felt a sense of accomplishment. I had been suspended from nursing because of my ex-husband's actions, and now I was about to start a new chapter with the Washington State Patrol. I hoped that, in this new role, I could help other families if they ever had to face a similar horror.

Once inside Clint's office, he sat Bridget down and gently encouraged her to write her statement. I could see he was sympathetic towards her, knowing the ordeal she'd been through with both Jared and Heath.

As she wrote, Clint turned to me and asked to speak with me privately in the other room.

"I'll be right back Bridge," I told my daughter.

"That's fine, mom," she said. And I knew she meant it. It would take time, but she was going to be okay.

Clint led me across the hall to a little break room, where a soda machine hummed quietly. I turned back so I could watch Bridget through the windows.

Before he could speak, a burning question spilled from my mouth. "There's something I don't get. When Jared called, why'd he say 'girls'? He said something like, 'I took the girls from their nests like I had been ripped from mine. Kept them in a cage.

One I let fly free. The one you know won't be so lucky.' The second one was Bridget. But if Heath was the killer, who was the other girl?"

"Heath's daughter."

My eyes went wide as Clint told me the story, which had spilled from Jared's lips straight into the notebook of the detective who'd met with him when he was let out of surgery.

CHAPTER 48

JARED HAD BEEN TELLING the truth. Heath had been the Waxlace Strangler all along.

He'd had suspicions immediately, but, while in prison, Jared had concluded that Heath stole his skates and strangled those girls. The blood on the laces had come from Jared's broken wrist. When he was released, Jared tracked down Heath and abducted his daughter to use as collateral.

Hiding Heath's daughter in the cabin at the bird sanctuary, he'd told Heath he would let her go if he killed again, if he revived the role of the Waxlace Strangler one more time. Jared chose Buck Lake Park in Hansville because he planned for me to become involved. He tried to warn us. In his warped mind, calling me and the police would be enough to have us catch Heath in the act, clearing his name forever without anyone getting hurt.

Unfortunately, I didn't get the message and emergency services chalked it up to a hoax after not finding anything on a few passes through Buck Lake Park.

Part of him, Jared had admitted, just wanted to clear his name. Another part wanted Heath to suffer in prison as he had.

Not as much for killing the girls, but more so for stealing his ice skates all those years ago.

When authorities didn't catch Heath in the act, Jared took Bridget, a final, desperate attempt to make me write a story, proving his innocence.

Heath had shown up at the cabin with the ice skates hoping to frame Jared. Apparently, killing Cara had sparked something in Heath. So, when Heath saw Bridget, he saw another opportunity to kill. He couldn't resist the urge.

Why did Heath Spencer kill the first girls in the first place? We still didn't know. My guess was that it would come down to something as simple—and as evil—as wounded pride. Maybe they'd rejected his advances, or made fun of him at the rink. In my mind, it didn't matter much now. Lawyers would be haggling over that bastard's fate for years. But my work was done. The Waxlace Strangler was off the streets and far from Buck Lake.

I was safe. I had my daughter.

But the other mothers... Nancy McDonald and the three from twenty years ago...

Being a nurse—and having seen losses of all kinds—this kind of loss was the worst.

People's children should never die first. That *should* be the rule.

As for the parents of those four girls, their lives had been ruined *forever.*

While leaning in to hear Clint's story, I noticed something that I hadn't seen before. Just to the left of Clint's neck there was a dark pink area on his skin, a scar barely peeking out from under his collar. Once I noticed it, I couldn't look away. Clint caught me staring and pulled away the neckline of his shirt to reveal what looked like it must have been a deep and wide gash. It ran from the base of his neck and followed along underneath his clavicle, nearly to his armpit.

"Wow," I said.

"Yeah, get a good look at it."

"What's it from?" I asked.

"Mistakes," Clint said. "But, like I already said, I don't talk about my past."

"Right," I said. "I remember your one rule."

Clint's face changed. "Listen, I didn't bring you in here to detail the case. Or to tell you about my past."

"Why *did* you bring me in here?" I asked.

His look was sad, almost embarrassed, his tone stern. "Anything *you* need to tell *me*, Macy? About *your* recent past?"

I stared at him, mind blank. There were probably a million things I needed to tell him, but he seemed to be referring to something specific.

I shrugged.

"There's an issue with your nursing license. Do you know what I'm talking about?"

My face immediately flushed red.

"So you *do* know," Clint said. "Did you know when you signed on?"

"I had been meaning to tell you there could be an issue." My speech was hurried, a pathetic lie. "It wasn't me who took those medications in the first place, and..."

"Look," Clint interrupted. "I had to peel Jacqueline from the ceiling when she found out." Clint lifted his eyebrows and rubbed the back of his neck.

"*She* knows, too?"

"She didn't hear it from me. They brought the info to her while processing your new hire paperwork. And, she left me a number of angry calls that went straight to voicemail while we were going after Bridget. I found out from Kenny. He told me he'd gotten your nursing license suspended, told me that he had taken medications from your patients and you had nothing to do with it."

"Kenny admitted everything?"

"He did," Clint confirmed. "I just left The Iron Chief's office. Took me some time to get her calmed down. Because, look, it's a legal thing. Forensic nurse has to be, 'ya know, a nurse with a license in good standing. And I'm sure you knew that."

"I did, and I'm sorry." A wave of guilt washed over me. My reasoning had seemed sound at the time, but the truth was, I knew what I was doing and knew it was wrong.

Clint's tone softened. "I explained to her that Kenny confessed. That without you, Carlo might've died. Without you, the Waxlace Strangler might still be at large. As far as I'm concerned, what you did led to justice being served, so I'm not losing sleep over a wrongfully suspended license. I don't need any bureaucratic BS telling me how to do my job. It took me some time to convince her." He paused, then met my eyes, his face breaking out in a rare smile. "Chief is wary, but willing to keep you on."

"Wait..." I looked at Clint, a shocked smile spreading across my face. "So I still have a job?"

"Tentatively so, yes. But, you will be on probation for quite some time. And you'll have to go through whatever process is needed to turn Kenny's confession into a valid license."

I nearly jumped up and hugged him, but instead I just reached out to shake his hand. "Thank you for advocating for me. I really see myself being able to make a positive impact here. I want to be part of this team."

Clint smiled again. "Your determination and tenacious mind will be a great asset."

I felt a spark of pride at his words and glanced at Bridget. I saw her quietly working on her statement in the room across the hall.

Clint let me go and I went back in the room to be with my girl. "We'll get through this, Bridget," I whispered, my hand resting on her shoulder. "We're tougher than nails, and we have each other."

Bridget nodded, tears shimmering in her eyes as she continued to write. I squeezed her shoulder reassuringly.

Clint handed me the paperwork to fill out a report as well. Someone else would assess Bridget for injury, but Clint wanted me to get a sense of the paperwork I would be using routinely.

"Don't get too into the forensic findings, Macy," Clint said. "I want you to fill this out like a mother, not like a nurse."

It was a standard nursing form, patient information, incident details, physical assessment and any medical care or treatments provided. I filled out what I could.

When Bridget had finished the paperwork, she stared blankly at the papers in front of her, her hand shaking slightly. "What's gonna happen to dad?" The thought of her father going to jail seemed to push Bridget to a point beyond tears.

Seeing her like this broke my heart, but I knew she needed strength, not pity. I leaned in, holding her gaze, and said gently yet firmly, "I'm not gonna lie… possibly jail. It's gonna be hard. But we can do hard things. *You* can do hard things."

Bridget's eyes flickered with recognition as she took a deep breath. "You're right, Mom. I just... it's so overwhelming."

"I know it is, sweetheart. But we'll face it together, one *kick* at a time."

"That *was* one hell of a kick, wasn't it?"

"I'll never forget the look on that bastard's face when you kicked him out of his own Porsche." I chuckled. "He looked like one of those squishy dolls you had when you were a girl. Eyes popping out as you busted his gut." I stroked her hair. "Well done, Bridge."

Finally, with our reports completed, Clint, Bridget, and I prepared to leave the station. As we walked out, we passed the conference room with the particle board table.

I came to a sudden stop when I saw Maria kneeling before

Carlo, like she was about to propose. Carlo sat in his wheelchair, his broken leg extended straight ahead like a suspended karate kick, aimed directly at her face. It was *a scene worth a gawk*, as my mother would say.

"Will you marry me?" Maria asked in the most sincere and sweet voice I had ever heard.

Carlo, however, responded with a teasing grin, "Actually, I'm interested in a friend of yours."

They both burst into laughter, and Clint and I exchanged glances before joining in. The laughter was a needed release, shaking off the tension of the past few days.

Bridget, however, looked stunned by the exchange. "Wow, that's harsh," she whispered to me, her brow furrowed.

I put my arm around her and replied, "Sweetie, this is true love."

"I don't get it," Bridget said, still confused as she looked from me to Clint.

"Oh, it's an inside joke." Clint smiled warmly and said, "You had to be there."

"But, I'm glad you weren't," I added.

CHAPTER 49

THE SUN DIPPED LOW, casting a golden glow across the whitecaps of the Puget Sound. I sat on the deck of my parents' waterfront house, sipping a glass of chardonnay and marveling at the picturesque view. I needed this moment of serenity.

It had been ten days since we had Bridget back in our arms, and I was still working on getting things back to... well, not *normal*. My old normal was gone for good, but I was well on my way to establishing a new one.

"Mom, these scalloped potatoes are gonna get cold," Bridget called from the dining room.

"Coming!" I hollered back, mentally saying goodbye to the peaceful scene. I rose from the deck chair, brushing off my jeans, and re-entered the house.

My mother had outdone herself with dinner. The long wooden table was laden with a savory feast: honey-glazed ham with mustard sauce, garlic-infused green beans, warm rolls that smelled like a bakery, and her famous scalloped potatoes, a dish that would make even the staunchest dieter throw caution to the wind.

My mother fussed over the arrangement of the plates, her

warm smile masked her age while her graying hair divulged it. "Don't forget the sauce, Macy," she reminded me as she handed me the boat to carry out to the table.

I shot her a grin. "As if I could ever forget your honey-mustard sauce, ma."

Just then, my grandmother came shuffling in from next door, her walker squeaking across the hardwood floor. Her wispy white hair framed a face full of wrinkles, like a roadmap of her life.

"Glad you could make it, Grandma," I said, giving her a gentle hug.

"Wouldn't miss it for the world," she replied, her voice still strong despite her age.

We settled into our seats, four generations of women, and began to pass around the dishes. As I piled my plate high with the mouthwatering meal, Gonzo whined at our feet. I couldn't decide if his red collar with bow tie made him look sophisticated or stupid. Either way, now I could be reached by whoever had the fortitude to pick him up. *And* could keep hold of him long enough to read my number engraved into the dog-bone-shaped tag that swung from his neck.

Gonzo deserved a treat, too, but it would have to wait until the rest of us were done dining. *Dorothy's house rules for dogs.*

"So, Mom," Bridget began, "I've been meaning to ask you something. Where did that *Notice Everything* saying come from? I remember stealing that sweatshirt from you, but I can't remember the exact story."

I looked up from my plate, wiping my mouth with a napkin. "Well, it came from my great-grandmother, your great-great-grandmother. She was a nurse, too. Her first job was in the Civil War, if you can believe that. 'Notice Everything' was her motto."

Ethel pointed a gnarled finger towards the ceiling, nodding sagely. "That's the first thing they ought to teach you in nursing school. Notice everything."

"That's right, Grandma," I agreed, passing the green beans to Bridget. "Your great-great-grandmother had a wall hanging with that embroidered on it, hanging in her living room."

We continued to eat and chat, sharing memories and laughter. I savored the flavors of the food, the warmth of my family, and the safety of being home.

"You know," I mused, twirling ham at the end of my fork, "that saying has stuck with me through the years."

My mom's blue eyes twinkled as she took a slow sip of water. "Well, dear, that's the key to life, isn't it? Noticing the little things—the good and the bad—so you can navigate the bigger picture."

Ethel leaned in, a mischievous glint in her eye. "Macy, why don't you tell Bridget about the time I carried that leg to the morgue?"

Bridget's eyes widened and she set her fork down. "Wait a second. Is this one of those 'I walked to school uphill both ways' kind of stories?"

I chuckled, glancing at my grandmother. "Yes, but walking uphill both ways carrying an amputated leg. Right, Grandma?"

My mom jumped in to fill in the details. "Mom went to nursing school in New York City in the fifties. They'd give you the scariest thing to do to see if you had the right stuff. You carried that leg all the way through the underground tunnels to the hospital, didn't you, Mom?"

Ethel nodded, her face a mix of pride and amusement. "I had to take two breaks leaning that leg against the wall. It felt like miles to get to the morgue."

I turned to Bridget, the story still vivid in my mind. "Grandma taught me to notice everything."

"Yes, notice everything, sweetie," Ethel said, her voice soft but firm.

"It served me well when I was a journalist, and even more so as a nurse," I continued. "Notice what you see and hear on your way down the hallway to your patient. Notice what you see, notice what you feel with your hands and with your heart. Then, do something with the information. If something smells, sounds, or feels wrong, do something about it. If something is right, speak to it. Look for, listen to, smell, and feel the beautiful things. Then share them. That's how to be a good nurse."

Bridget looked thoughtful, her gaze drifting toward the window and the beautiful view outside. "I'll remember that, Mom. It's good advice for nursing and for life in general."

I reached across the table and squeezed her hand.

Bridget looked up from her plate, a curious expression on her face. "Is Pa coming down for dinner?"

"He's up in the shop," my mom replied, shaking her head with a knowing smile.

I echoed her sentiment. "He's always up in the shop."

"Quiet everyone!" Bridget dramatically pointed a finger into the air and shifted her eye from side to side. "I don't hear any power tools." She inhaled deeply through her nose. "But, I don't smell any diesel fuel yet. Notice everything, right, Grandma Ethel?"

My grandmother coughed weakly after a hard swallow, then managed a smile. "Yes, my girl. Notice everything."

Dorothy glanced toward the stairs. "If we don't hear him and we don't smell him, that means he's on his way down. He'll head straight to the shower if he knows what's good for him, and then I'll warm up his meal."

As we continued to eat, the conversation shifted to Kenny, who'd gotten out on bail. His lawyer was saying that he might not even do jail time, since his theft was for personal use due to opioid addiction, rather than for resale. Plus, he was a first-time offender and had voluntarily entered a treatment program.

We talked about how it was time for all of us to forgive him, at least to the extent that we could have him over for dinner sometime. My soft spot for Bridget's father was no secret, and I knew that healing those old wounds was important.

"Why don't we have dinner again tomorrow night?" my mother asked. "Kenny can come, too."

I hesitated, then admitted, "I can't make it tomorrow. I have a date."

At that moment, the smell of diesel fuel wafted through the house. My dad walked through the room wearing his dirty overalls.

He raised his arms in the air and crossed his fingers as he walked by. "Please don't say it's with Kenny," he pleaded. "Please don't say it's with Kenny."

CHAPTER 50

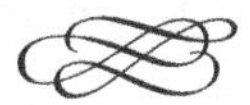

THE NEXT DAY, I stood outside the auto repair shop waiting for Frank. I leaned against the brick wall, the sun casting long shadows over the pavement, and sighed. It was the last time I'd ever be there as the owner, and the reality of it was absolutely freeing.

As I rattled the keys in my hand, Frank's customized hot rod rumbled into view. The re-built '67 Camarro had a high-performance engine and custom exhaust system. The car emitted a thunderous roar and its metallic blue color and silver racing stripes made it even more electrifying. The black leather interior was set against brushed aluminum details that shimmered in the sunlight.

It came to a stop in front of the shop, and Frank hopped out with a wide grin. "Hey, Mac!" he called, giving me a friendly wave. "Bought myself this little peach. I've been sober for over a week and plan to keep it that way."

I wanted to say something snarky, but I managed an encouraging, "Good for you, Frank."

I held out the keys.

Frank took them from my hand and inspected them.

"What's this one for?" he asked, holding up the diamond-shaped key.

Turned out, Frank actually *had* inherited a quarter million dollars from an aunt. And he'd agreed to buy The Wrench King for $10,000, plus all the money needed to pay off its debts. I still had personal debts to deal with, but this was a decent start. I was throwing in the contents of the storage container as a bonus.

"Oh, there are some tools and spare parts and stuff in a storage unit in downtown Kingston. Some nice seats, too. Take anything you like. You have another week before they throw everything out, I'm about to end the lease."

"What's with the diamond key shape?" he asked.

"You ever heard of shinola?"

"Sure have. One man's shinola is another man's treasure."

I rubbed the back of my neck, thinking about how I could politely end this conversation with as little awkwardness as possible. "Well..." I started.

"Bittersweet day, huh?" Frank interrupted.

"You could say that." I nodded, glancing at the shop, then back at Frank. "I guess I have put a lot of blood, sweat, and tears into this place over the years."

Frank's expression softened. "I know. And I promise, I'm gonna take good care of it. And your Cabriolet too. I'll fix it up for you. Whenever you need. On the house."

I managed a smile, but inside I was torn.

I couldn't figure out which I wanted less: to set foot in The Wrench King ever again, or to let that man near my precious Ice Cream.

LATER THAT EVENING, I found myself at a waterfront bistro in Poulsbo, overlooking the marina. The evening sun cast a warm glow over the boats bobbing in the water. As I sat, I breathed deeply, savoring the salty breeze that rustled through my hair.

Pulling out my phone, I sent a quick text to Bridget, just to check in. She responded with a reassuring thumbs-up emoji, which made me smile.

A sudden shadow fell over the table, and I looked up to see my date. My pulse quickened at the sight of him.

Jason, the hot EMT I'd reconnected with the night that Bob died, wore a casual light blue button-down shirt and bluejeans, his strong build evident beneath the fabric.

"Hey, Macy," he said, flashing a warm smile as he took the seat across from me.

"Hey, Jason."

"You look amazing tonight, Macy."

I'd spent $100 of Frank's ten grand on a new black dress for the occasion. "Thanks." I felt my cheeks flush, but I grinned back at him. "I didn't know EMTs had such good fashion sense."

He chuckled, his eyes crinkling at the corners. "Well, we can't wear uniforms all the time, can we?"

As the evening unfolded, our conversation flowed effortlessly. I told Jason about my new job with the WSP and about the case I'd just been a part of. He'd read pieces of it in the local newspapers, but I gave him all the details.

At the end of our meal, we sat slowly sipping wine and trading lighter stories about our jobs, our families, and our dreams. Laughter filled the space between us, and I found myself thinking that this could be the beginning of something.

"I can't believe you asked me out after seeing me in those pajamas," I said. "I wouldn't want to be caught dead in those rags."

He smiled at me and leaned in. "Unfortunately," he whispered. "I've seen people who've been caught dead wearing worse, may they rest in peace."

"Given your line of work, I'm sure you have," I said. "May they rest in peace, indeed."

"You know, Macy, this isn't a pity date or anything. You aren't scaring me away with your goofy ways. You might not like to admit it but, you're cute as hell. I like you. Honest."

"Here's to my goofy ways, then." I held up a glass and he met my toast.

Now that I knew how he felt about goofy women, I wondered how he might feel about tyrannical chihuahuas and crippling debt.

"Hey," Jason said, "I've got tickets to the Seahawks game next Monday night. Opening night. Monday night football. The weather is supposed to be great. Wanna go?"

"Sure do," I said. "I could use a bit of great weather."

It had been a rough couple weeks, but everything was about to get better.

—The End—

If you enjoyed *The Girl in Area One,* please check out the next book in the series online. It's called *The Man at Pier Two.*

ABOUT THE AUTHOR

Eva Blue resides in a picturesque beach town near Seattle with her husband (mystery author D.D. Black), their two spirited children, and other animals including a precious Corgi named Pearl, an old rescue mutt named Chester, and a neurotic Chihuahua mix named Buffy, who reigns supreme.

As a third-generation nurse on her maternal side, Eva was heavily influenced by watching *Unsolved Mysteries* with her father and *Murder, She Wrote* with her grandmother. Raised in part by Golden Retrievers, Eva's love of dogs and fascination with archetypal human stories led her to create these gripping tales featuring her brilliant and sassy protagonist, Macy Ellis. In *The Macy Puget Sound Mysteries,* heroines stand strong, fearlessly facing formidable foes—both human and otherwise.

Step into Eva Blue's thrilling realm of cunning villains, tenacious women and men, and mind-bending twists that will keep you on the edge of your seat.

Connect with Eva on Facebook and join her ever-growing community of mystery lovers.

WHAT TO READ NEXT

The next Macy Ellis Puget Sound mystery is called *The Man at Pier Two* and it's scheduled to be released in September, 2023.

While you're waiting, I encourage you to check out my husband's fabulous mystery series, *The Thomas Austin Crime Thrillers*:

Book 1: *The Bones at Point No Point*

Book 2: *The Shadows of Pike Place*

Book 3: *The Fallen of Foulweather Bluff*

Book 4: *The Horror at Murden Cove*

Book 5: The Terror in The Emerald City

Book 6: The Drowning at Dyes Inlet

Made in the USA
Monee, IL
31 January 2024